Alex heard something, a muffled cough-gasp that echoed from across the room. The closet.

He slowly crossed the room, then whipped the door open. He reached up, pulled the light chain and spotted a woman cowering behind a stack of boxes. Her face was buried in arms folded across her knees.

"Miss?" He crouched in front of her. "It's okay, I'm Detective Alex Donovan."

She didn't look up.

Alex spotted a cell phone clenched in her hand. She must have made the 9-1-1 call.

"Are you a friend of Edward Lange?"

A negative head shake.

"Do you work for him?"

She nodded affirmative.

"Were you here when he was attacked?"

She nodded yes. He wanted to tell her it was going to be okay, but he wasn't one to make promises he couldn't keep. If she was hiding in here, that meant she might have seen or heard something that could help them find the killer—and consequently put her life in danger.

Books by Hope White

Love Inspired Suspense

Hidden in Shadows
Witness on the Run
Christmas Haven
Small Town Protector
Safe Harbor

HOPE WHITE

An eternal optimist, Hope White was born and raised in the Midwest. She began spinning tales of intrigue and adventure when she was in grade school, and wrote her first book when she was eleven—a thriller that ended with a mysterious phone call the reader never heard!

She and her college sweetheart have been married for thirty years and are blessed with two wonderful sons, two feisty cats and a bossy border collie.

When not dreaming up inspirational tales, Hope enjoys hiking, sipping tea with friends and going to the movies. She loves to hear from readers, who can contact her at hopewhiteauthor@gmail.com.

SAFE HARBOR

HOPE
WHITE

H **HARLEQUIN**® LOVE INSPIRED® SUSPENSE

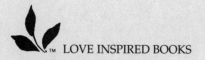 LOVE INSPIRED BOOKS

Recycling programs
for this product may
not exist in your area.

ISBN-13: 978-0-373-18571-9

SAFE HARBOR

Copyright © 2013 by Pat White

www.LoveInspiredBooks.com

Printed in U.S.A.

Therefore, as God's chosen people, holy and dearly loved, clothe yourselves with compassion, kindness, humility, gentleness and patience.
—*Colossians* 3:12

To Anio, for a lifetime of friendship

ONE

Personal assistant Nicole Harris dropped her messenger bag on the floor next to Mr. Lange's desk and answered her cell phone. "This is Nicole."

"Thank you so much for covering for me this weekend," her boss, Ruby said. "I owe you."

"Big time." Nicole smiled, logged into Outlook and sorted piles of papers on the computer magnate's desk. Edward Lange may be a tech genius but he had the organizational skills of a five-year-old on a sugar high.

"I just can't do weekends, not with the boys' soccer and baseball and—"

"Hey, no problem." Nicole didn't have a husband or family so she didn't mind working on the weekend, especially if it meant helping out her boss, who'd also become a good friend.

"What can I do to repay you?" Ruby asked.

"It's my job, remember?"

"And you're seriously good at it or Edward wouldn't have requested you. Did you get the passcodes I texted you earlier?"

"Yes, ma'am. Committed them to memory and ate my phone."

"Very funny."

The front door slammed.

"He's back from his run. Gotta go." Nic pocketed her phone and checked Mr. Lange's Outlook calendar to make sure he wasn't missing anything crucial by escaping the city on a whim. Nic was a natural at her job as a personal assistant, but then she'd spent her childhood keeping her younger sister and brother organized.

Voices echoed down the front hallway. Odd, considering she was told they weren't expecting guests this weekend. She blocked out the voices and focused on checking messages on Mr. Lange's smartphone.

"It's borderline criminal!" Mr. Lange shouted.

Shouted? He was usually such a soft-spoken man. Nic felt guilty eavesdropping, so she refocused on his voice mails. "Mr. Lange, this is Audrey Ross from *Tech Worldwide*. I'm on a deadline and I need a statement about the Tech-Link software failure—"

"I said no!"

Her shoulders jerked.

"It's okay, it's not him," she coached herself, as posttraumatic panic skittered across her nerve endings.

Something slammed against the wall, rattling the books in the mahogany case next to the door. She slowly backed up toward the closet.

"Get out of my house!" Mr. Lange bellowed.

Her pulse raced as buried memories of her abusive father rushed to the surface.

"I said out!"

She darted into the closet and shut the door with a soft click. Scrambling to the far corner, she hid behind a stack of boxes.

Some part of her brain realized how ridiculous it would look when Mr. Lange found his personal assistant huddled in the closet, but her reaction was automatic. She couldn't make another choice if her life depended on it.

"You need to reconsider," a second man said, his voice higher pitched and more clear.

They'd entered the office.

"Nothing is going to change my mind," Mr. Lange said.

Something slammed against the closet door. She bit back a squeak and hugged her knees to her chest.

"Why are you still here?" Mr. Lange accused.

"Because you haven't called the cops."

"The only reason I haven't called the cops is because of my—"

A soft pop made her gasp. Then another.

A gunshot? No, it couldn't be.

Silence rang in her ears. She focused on breathing so she wouldn't pass out.

The sound of breaking glass echoed through the door, then swearing, and more crashing. She hugged her knees tighter, fisted her hands.

She squeezed her eyes shut.

Waited.

It was just a matter of time before he opened the closet door.

Flashes of her childhood paralyzed her, rendering her unable to think clearly.

Hide in the corner. Be quiet and still, she'd coach Beau and Addy.

She had to do something, call the police, a friend, someone. Instead, she huddled in tighter, losing all sense of time and place as the memories closed in.

Then the door opened...

Detective Alex Donovan knew something was off the minute he entered Edward Lange's study. Instinct twisted his gut as he scanned the room.

"Chief Roth and the coroner are on the way," officer Mark Adams said, standing in the doorway.

Alex crouched to look at the room from another angle, wrestling with the frustration building in his chest.

Edward Lange. Dead.

The entrepreneur-philanthropist often came to Waverly Harbor to get away from the intensity of the city, demands of his work and the relentless media. When he bought the lake house three years ago, he'd asked for a meeting with Chief Roth and his staff to discuss his residing in their small town. Although community members knew about the purchase of the lake house, they'd agreed to give Lange his privacy and help him avoid the spotlight. In return he'd generously donated money to build a new community center and library. He didn't have to make those donations. Folks of Waverly Harbor were nothing if not protective, and they had embraced Lange as one of their own without expecting anything in return.

"His driver is outside," Mark Adams said.

"He called it in?"

"No. He claims he was outside in the car and didn't hear anything. The call came from Lange's cell."

Alex went to the body, careful not to disturb the crime scene. Not easy with the clutter of papers littering the floor. Someone was looking for something.

Alex crouched again, eyed the area around

Edward's face, and down to his hands. "There's no phone near the body."

"Maybe the intruder took it?"

Alex studied Edward Lange's face. "Where's your security?" he whispered.

No bodyguards and the alarm wasn't set? Which meant what? That Edward knew his attacker. Was the killer a personal friend or staff member?

Alex scanned the immediate area and spotted a gold chain-link bracelet, a man's wallet and pair of sunglasses on the floor near the body.

"You want to talk to—"

Alex put up two fingers to silence the cop. He thought he heard something, a faint whimper, but he couldn't be sure.

He closed his eyes, blocked out his surroundings, and listened.

A muffled cough-gasp echoed from across the room. The closet.

Alex withdrew his firearm, slowly crossed the room and motioned for Mark to open the door on the count of three.

One, two, three.

Mark whipped the door open and Alex

heard a squeak. Aiming his firearm into the dark closet, he reached up and pulled the light chain. He spotted a female, Caucasian with flaming red hair, cowering behind a stack of boxes. He holstered his gun and stepped closer for a better look. Her face was buried in arms folded across her knees. She was a trembling mass of red from her hair to her red blouse, down to her red tennis shoes.

"Miss?" He crouched in front of her. "It's okay, I'm Detective Alex Donovan."

She didn't look up.

"Can you tell us what happened?" he tried.

She shook her head *no*.

"Can you tell me your name?"

She shook her head *no* again.

Alex glanced at Mark. "Look for a purse or briefcase with ID."

Mark disappeared from the doorway.

Alex spotted a cell phone clenched in her hand. She must have made the 911 call.

"Are you a friend of—" He was about to say the deceased and caught himself. "Edward Lange?"

Another negative head shake.

"Do you work for him?"

She nodded affirmative.

"Were you here when he was attacked?"

She nodded yes, her body trembling slightly. He wanted to place a comforting hand on her shoulder, tell her it was going to be okay, but he wasn't one to make promises he couldn't keep. If she was hiding in here that meant she might have seen or heard something that could help them find the killer—and consequently put her life in danger.

"Alex?" Mark said, stepping into the closet. "Found this by the desk." He placed a messenger bag next to Alex and handed him a purple leather wallet. Alex pulled out a driver's license that read *Nicole Desiree Harris*.

Voices echoed through the house. The coroner must have arrived, and then some. Alex had a feeling everyone would want to be involved in this investigation, including state and county law enforcement. Edward was an influential man, a celebrity of sorts.

"Can you keep them out of here for a few minutes?" Alex asked Mark.

"I'll do my best."

Alex put the wallet in the messenger bag and redirected his attention to Miss Harris, pushing back the temptation to pick her up and carry her to a safe, quiet place.

"Miss Harris, it's going to get awfully loud in here as more police personnel show up. How about I take you to another room where it's quiet?"

She slowly raised her head and pinned him with brilliant amber-colored eyes. He stopped breathing for a second, so affected by the devastation he read there.

"Nice to meet you," he recovered, and extended his hand, figuring he had to try.

She studied it for a second, then reached out and accepted his gesture. Her trembling fingers were cold and fragile as she clasped his hand. And he prayed to God that he could do right by this one.

She searched his eyes as if wanting to say something but couldn't get the words out.

Male voices boomed from the outlying office and her fingers squeezed his hand.

"Let's get you out of here." He stood and helped her up. She was petite, probably five-three, and a floral scent drifted from her hair.

"It's okay. No one's going to hurt you." He positioned her on his left side so when they walked out of the closet she wouldn't be assaulted by the bloody image of Edward Lange.

She hugged her midsection with her free arm, but wouldn't let go of his right hand. He put his left arm around her shoulder to shield her from the frenetic crime scene.

"Is this okay?" he said.

She nodded that it was, grabbed her messenger bag and flung it over her shoulder.

Someone barked an order from the office and her shoulders jerked.

"See what I mean? Loud," he said.

As he led her out of the closet, the half dozen men froze at the sight of Alex and Miss Harris deliberately crossing the room.

"Detective Donovan, I think—"

"Don't," Alex snapped.

He didn't know who'd spoken and didn't care. Alex needed to get the witness out of this room and away from the violent scene as quickly as possible. As they passed, all eyes were on the red-haired, traumatized beauty. She kept her head down, eyes focused on the carpet a few feet in front of her.

They crossed the threshold into the hallway and he spotted pocket doors. Hopefully he could find another room with pocket doors so he could close her off from the chaos.

He escorted her down the hall to a TV room in the back of the house and slid the pocket doors shut.

"How's this?" He led her to a thick-cushioned sofa.

She sat down, still clinging to his hand, so he sat next to her. He wanted to be out there assisting with the crime scene, but he wouldn't leave her alone. Maybe they could call a female sheriff's deputy to keep her company. Surely a woman would be better at comforting a terrified female witness.

Clutching his hand, she sighed and leaned against his shoulder. For a brief second it reminded him of Jessica, how she'd leaned against him when they'd watched movies. Despair ripped through Alex's chest, followed by guilt.

Get your head in the game, Alex.

This woman's life could be in danger, which meant the sooner they found the killer the sooner she'd be safe.

"Is he…dead?"

Her voice was throaty, deeper than he'd imagined.

"Yes," he answered.

She shook her head and a tear trailed down her cheek. He nearly reached out to wipe it away, but caught himself.

"Was there anyone else in the house besides you, Mr. Lange and the intruder?"

"Not that I know of."

"No bodyguards?"

"No."

Which puzzled Alex because he thought bodyguards followed Lange everywhere.

"Can you talk about what happened, Miss Harris?" he asked.

She shook her head. A few minutes passed in companionable silence. It had been a long time since Alex held a woman like this. He didn't have much interest in romance after Jessica's death.

"Nicole," she said, breaking the silence.

"Please call me Nicole." She clung to her messenger bag in her lap. "I wasn't supposed to be here."

"Then why *were* you here?"

"I'm a personal assistant. I was filling in for a friend."

"Had you worked with Mr. Lange before?"

"Yes."

"But you're not his regular assistant?"

She shook her head *no*.

"Did you hear what happened?"

She squeezed his hand, but didn't answer. He should have known it was too soon to ask, but the killer was out there, maybe still on the property if he hadn't found what he was looking for in Edward's office.

Alex wouldn't push Nicole. Most of the time if you pushed a witness they either pushed back or shut down completely. He felt lucky she was talking to him after what she'd just experienced.

They gazed out the back window at the lake, the setting sun peeking through the evergreens in the distance.

The pocket door slid open, breaking the peaceful moment. A man in a dark suit, white shirt and maroon tie marched across the room, blocking their view. The guy looked like a Fed.

"This the witness?" the suit demanded.

"And you are?" Alex countered.

"Special Agent Richard Banks with the FBI," he said, flashing his ID. The stern-faced, broad-shouldered agent was in his mid-forties, and definitely all business.

"What's the FBI's interest in this case?" Alex asked.

"We'll discuss that later. So, this is Nicole Harris?"

"Yes." Alex wished Banks would lower the volume a few notches.

Instead, he directed his attention to Nicole. "Ma'am, can you tell me what happened tonight?"

She shook her head and stared out the window with a detached expression. Banks studied her as if trying to determine if her shock was real or an act.

"You found her in the closet?" he asked Alex.

"Yes."

"Did she hear anything?"

"She hasn't been able to talk about it."

Banks clenched his jaw and glared at Nicole.

"Did the driver see anything?" Alex redirected.

"One of my agents is interviewing him."

"What about the bodyguards? Where were they?" Alex said.

"Don't know. The house is empty except for the witness and the victim. It's imperative that I interview her ASAP."

"She's obviously not ready to talk about it."

"When *will* she be able to talk about it?"

The guy was being a class A jerk. Alex glanced at Nicole. She still stared blindly out the window, her cheeks even more pale than they were a minute ago.

"I don't have time for this," Banks said. "Ma'am, you'll need to come with me, if nothing else, for your own protection."

The guy seriously needed a crash course in sensitivity.

She snapped her attention to Agent Banks. "My protection? Do you think he'll come after me? But I didn't...see anything."

"The murderer doesn't know that and he won't stop until—"

"Enough," Alex interrupted. "Agent Banks, can we talk in the hallway?"

Banks marched out of the room and Alex turned to Nicole. "I'll just be a minute, okay?"

Yet he was hesitant to let go of her hand. What was it about this woman?

Simple. She was in danger and Alex was a natural-born protector. Maybe this time he'd get it right. Maybe this one wouldn't die because of his incompetence.

"I'll be right back." He slipped his hand from hers and stood.

She hugged herself. "You think… Will he…come after me?"

Seeing fear in her eyes, he mustered up the only answer he thought might ease her anxiety. "I doubt he even knew you were there. You found a clever hiding spot."

She nodded, but didn't look convinced.

As he headed toward the hallway to speak to Agent Banks, Alex focused on controlling the frustration burning through his chest. Intimidating Nicole was no way to get answers, not to mention it was incredibly inappropriate behavior for a professional.

Alex went into the hallway. Agent Banks took a step toward him. "What do you think you're doing?"

"I'm trying to make the witness feel safe so she'll talk to us," he answered in a calm voice.

"Well, she's obviously bonded with you."

"And that's a bad thing?"

"Was that your plan? To play hero?" the agent accused.

"This isn't about being a hero. It's about finding a killer."

Banks slammed his fist against the wall and leaned close. "I heard about you and your wonder-boy reputation on the Denver force. I won't allow ego to mess up this investigation."

"I guarantee you, *my* ego won't be a problem."

Alex stood his ground, refusing to back down. He surely wasn't going to let Agent Banks take Nicole in for questioning if he planned to continue these aggressive tactics on her.

With a frustrated expression, Banks turned and paced a few feet away.

"Are you going to tell me why the Feds are involved?" Alex asked.

"Edward Lange was a target of an ongoing investigation. I can't share the details."

"You suspect him of criminal activity?" Alex couldn't believe it.

Agent Banks turned to Alex. "Like I said, it's need-to-know information."

"If it'll help me solve the murder, then I need to know."

"That's not my call."

"Nor is it my call to release the witness into your custody. You'll have to take that up with my chief."

"I don't have time to cut through your local red tape, detective."

"You don't have a choice. The witness is traumatized and won't talk about what happened until she feels safe."

"And that's your job? To make her feel safe?" he said.

Alex ignored the attitude. "It's certainly my goal. But she won't be safe unless we work together and catch the perp. I can guarantee you that isolating her in an interrogation room isn't going to get you the answers you're looking for."

Banks ran his hand across his jawline. "You're right. There's just a lot riding on this case."

"My suggestion is we keep her identity a secret," Alex said. "Better yet, don't release the fact there *was* a witness. Can you talk to the first responders in there?"

"Yes, but you know how things leak out."

"It's worth a try. In the meantime, I'll take Miss Harris someplace safe. Here's my cell number." Alex handed him a business card. "I'd appreciate you keeping me in the loop on your end and I'll do the same."

Deep in thought, Banks glanced at Alex's business card.

"How bad is it, whatever you think Lange was into?" Alex pushed.

"It's a game changer." He handed Alex his business card and went back to the crime scene.

Officer Mark Adams stepped into the hallway looking for Alex. "How's the witness?"

"Understandably upset. I need you to keep

an eye on things here," Alex said. "I'm taking her into protective custody."

"Yes, sir."

Alex turned back to the TV room and took a deep breath. Somehow he had to convince Nicole Harris to shelve her trauma and tell them whatever she could about the murder. Time was critical, potentially for the community of Waverly Harbor but most definitely for Nicole. Alex knew it would be nearly impossible to keep her presence in town a secret, but he hoped they could keep it quiet that she'd been at the crime scene, sitting on the other side of the closet door while someone viciously murdered Edward Lange. If that got out, even by accident, it could mean Nicole's life.

No, he wouldn't let it happen again. He'd stay one step ahead of the killer and make sure an innocent woman didn't become a victim.

He slid the pocket doors open.

"We decided I should take you—" he said to an empty room. "Miss Harris? Nicole?"

He rushed to the sofa hoping to find her stretched out in exhaustion.

She was gone. So was her messenger bag.

He spotted a closet and raced across the room to whip open the door. Switched on the light.

Empty.

How was that possible? He bolted to the sliding door and whipped it open. "Nicole!"

TWO

She had to run.

There was no other choice.

The killer was after her. He wanted her dead. The FBI agent had said as much. And the only way to survive was to either hide…

Or run.

Because given Nic's experience, the police couldn't or wouldn't protect her. She was the only one who could save herself.

She'd hesitated before taking off, remembering the false sense of security she'd felt when leaning against the muscled arm of Detective Donovan. When he spoke in his rich, deep voice, she could almost believe the words coming out of his mouth, and she was sure she read truth in his striking blue eyes.

But then something had slammed against

the wall, snapping her out of her momentary distraction, yanking her back to reality and the violence that surrounded her.

No one can help you but yourself. A lesson learned years ago as a child.

Jogging across the property toward the lake, she figured the next house was about four city blocks away. She'd make her way there and…and…what?

Didn't matter, she couldn't think about what came next. She had to stay focused on getting away from the murder scene, the cops…the threat to her life.

She had to feel safe.

A sob-gasp caught in her throat. Safe? Since when?

In the recesses of her mind, her intellect argued that this was a bad move. She couldn't elude authorities for long and it could even make her look guilty, as if she'd done something wrong. Yet all she'd done was her job.

If she couldn't be safe in this quiet little town that meant…

He was right.

You can't run fast enough or hide well enough. You'll never be safe.

"No," she gasped, picking up speed as she eyed the lights of a house in the distance.

She was a survivor, a fighter. A killer had stood on the other side of a closet door, weapon in hand, yet she was still alive. The cops said they wanted to protect her but she knew the truth: they wanted something *from* her.

No one genuinely cared about Nicole, not even the polite and handsome Detective Donovan with the calming voice. She knew how it worked. She'd grown up the victim of a failed system, heard all the excuses about keeping children with their father, the one remaining parent. "A little discipline is no cause for putting the kids in foster care and splitting up a family," the caseworker had said.

In reality, "a little discipline" equated to extreme emotional abuse in the Harris household. Those scars weren't obvious, and her little sister and brother were so frightened of their dad that they wouldn't let on about the abuse to teachers, doctors or even friends. The kids feared his retaliation.

He'd earned that fear.

He'd leave newspaper articles on the kitchen counter about parents disciplining their children by locking them in a nonworking freezer in the backyard for two days, or locking them in a dog cage in the basement.

And being found dead.

Beau and Addy didn't want to be afraid all the time, but they didn't want to be dead, either, so Nicole taught them how to survive.

Tonight she needed those very survival tactics to escape the threat of a killer.

She must have run a quarter mile, her arms pumping, her brain spinning. Disappearing, then starting fresh in a new state with a new name was her best option. She'd planned for this day just in case the monster named Timothy Harris came looking for her.

She never thought she'd need the escape bag to flee a random killer.

Aiming for the cedar trees bordering the property, she thought she heard something behind her. Her name. Detective Donovan was calling her name.

She charged into the thick mass of trees for camouflage. If the police found her they'd take her into custody "for her own protection," while in fact they'd make her an easy target for a killer she hadn't even seen. Would she be able to identify his voice if she heard it again? She shoved the thought back. It didn't matter. She had no intention of putting herself in the line of fire.

Guilt snagged her conscience. What about Edward Lange? Didn't he deserve justice? Of course, but she hadn't seen anything and wasn't sure she'd recognize the voice if she heard it again.

Besides, this was about survival. It was always about survival.

She darted behind a towering cedar to catch her breath.

"Nicole Harris!" Detective Donovan shouted. He sounded frantic. The beam of a flashlight arced across the property, then skipped across the lake.

She slowly backed up, turned and—

Came face first with a chain-link security fence. She was locked in, with nowhere to go.

"No," she gasped.

"What's the matter?" a man said.

Startled, she spun around and eyed the surrounding trees but didn't see anyone.

"Who's there?"

Silence echoed back at her. Goose bumps shot down her arms. She scanned the area, looking for escape, but saw only darkness.

Suddenly a man stepped out from behind a tree, the brim of his baseball cap pulled low, shielding his face.

"I said, what's the matter?"

"Who are you?"

"Who are *you?*"

There was something about his voice, the way he lurked in the shadows and wouldn't identify himself, that set off a gazillion red flags in her brain.

Then he took a step toward her.

She took off, sprinting in the direction of the lake. Maybe not her smartest move but this had been a day of irrational decisions borne of fear.

If she could get out to the dock and wave her arms, cry out like a crazy person, Detective Donovan would see her, right? At this point she'd take the cops over a strange man with a creepy demeanor.

"Hey," the man called after her.

She kept running.

Aimed for the dock.

She wanted to scream, call out for help, but she needed every ounce of energy to breathe.

Was he close?

She glanced over her shoulder...and tripped on a tree root poking up from the ground. Her messenger bag slipped off her shoulder as she tumbled over the edge of the embankment into the water.

She squeezed her eyes shut against the pain of rocks digging into her back and legs. Her head slammed against something hard and she plunged into the water, her breath catching in her throat.

"Help!" she cried, although it sounded more like one of her cat's high-pitched squeaks. She treaded water, shaking her head to clear it of a buzzing sound.

The weight of her clothes pulled her down.

Her mind spun with panic.

Stupid, worthless moron.

They were her monster father's words, words that taunted her as she struggled to stay above the water's surface. Arms flailing, she fought for breath, for life.

She tried to call out.

Her vision blurred and the buzzing intensified.

Help, somebody help me.

Instead, the water swallowed her, pulling her into its chilling embrace.

Alex knew he heard a woman call out for help. "Nicole! Nicole Harris!"

Complete and utter silence answered him.

His heart pounded against his chest as he listened intently for the sound of distress.

Then he heard a splash.

He sprinted toward the lake and aimed his flashlight at the water, desperate to see a break in the calm surface.

He was on his own. No one knew Nicole had gone missing. Alex didn't have time to tell anyone in the house. He had to find her, make sure she was okay.

The silence ringing in his ears indicated she was not okay. Why did she run? He didn't get it. Unless she was involved in Edward's murder?

He refused to believe that. She wouldn't have been trembling in the closet if she'd been a part of the plan to kill him. She would have been long gone before authorities showed up.

"Nicole!" he called out.

He skimmed the water's surface with his flashlight.

If Nicole had no reason to run from the authorities, that meant...she'd been running from the killer?

"Nicole! Answer me!" he demanded, jogging along the shoreline to the small pier. Racing onto the wooden planks, he aimed his flashlight across the wet rocks by the shore and spotted her messenger bag. He pointed the beam out about ten feet from shore...

And spotted a break in the water.

A hand reached out, then sank below the surface.

"Not happening." He ripped off his jacket and firearm and tossed them on the wooden planks. He kicked off his boots and dove in.

His body cramped as he hit the frigid water, but it wasn't as if he had another option. Nicole had either fallen in or been pushed. She might drown if he didn't get to her.

Blackness surrounded him beneath the water's surface. He swung his arms in the hopes of making contact. Defeat taunted him, but he shoved it aside and kept flailing his arms in desperation.

And brushed up against something.

Someone.

With renewed strength he gripped her arm and kicked to the surface, pulling her with him. Rolling her onto her back, he placed an arm around her chest and swam toward the dock.

He was close, so close. He got to the dock ladder, hoisted her over his shoulder and climbed the metal steps. He laid her gently against the wooden planks.

He felt for a pulse.

She was alive, but not breathing. He started chest compressions. One, two, three, four…

No one's going to hurt you.

A promise he didn't intend to make and was unable to keep. Yet he couldn't have guessed she'd run out into the darkness. What had spooked her?

Finishing chest compressions, he tilted her head and performed mouth-to-mouth. She coughed, the best sound he'd heard in years, and he gently rolled her onto her side facing him. She retched twice and went still. She blinked a few times, turned her head and looked up at Alex.

"You're okay," he assured her.

So was Alex, thanks to her beautiful eyes staring back at him. She seemed dazed, and that's when he noticed redness forming above her left eye.

"What happened?" he said.

She touched her head. "I was running and tripped." Her amber eyes rounded with fear. "There was a man...it could have been the killer."

When she struggled to get up, Alex placed a comforting hand on her shoulder. "Sit tight for a second, okay?"

He scrambled across the pier and grabbed his radio. "Mark, it's Alex. Send officers out back to search the property. Miss Harris encountered an unidentified man. Could be our suspect. Over." He glanced back at Nicole. She trembled worse than when he'd found her in the closet. This time it wasn't just from fear. She could be suffering from hypothermia.

He yanked on his boots, clipped his firearm to his belt and grabbed his jacket. He laid it across her shoulders. "We've gotta get you into some dry clothes."

She stood and wavered, so he automatically scooped her up into his arms. "Are you okay with this?"

"Y-y-yeah."

Which was a good thing because nothing could make him let her go. He went to the embankment, grabbed her messenger bag off the ground and strode across the back lawn toward the side gate. Alex avoided trekking through the house with Nicole in his arms. FBI agents would surely stop him, asking more questions, demanding answers.

He didn't have time for that. He needed to get her somewhere safe. Nicole had almost been killed while he'd stood not a hundred feet away. Thanks to his keen senses he'd heard the splash in the water that could have been the last movement she made in this life.

Instead, he was carrying her shivering body in his arms. *Thank You, Lord, for helping me find her.*

Now he had to make good on his promise that no one would hurt her again.

"Were you staying at the lake house?" he asked.

She shook her head that she wasn't.

"Did you rent a room in town?"

She nodded that she had. She was back to nodding instead of speaking, which made sense considering she'd been so close to death twice now in the past few hours. Carrying her gently but firmly, he scanned the property as they headed toward the gate that led to the driveway.

Just as he nudged the gate aside with his boot, the sliding door opened in back of the house and men's voices drifted across the property. Alex focused on getting Nicole safely to his truck. Answers would have to come later, or even tomorrow, after she'd warmed up and Alex was confident she was out of physical danger.

Which brought up the question of why she ran in the first place.

"Why did you take off like that?" he asked.

"S-s-scared."

"In a house full of cops?"

She shook her head in dismissal, obviously not wanting to talk about it. Fine, they didn't have to discuss her reasons right now but after she thawed out he was getting answers as to why she put herself at risk.

Great, now he was starting to sound like the bully FBI agent.

"What happened?" A short man with black hair, in his mid-fifties ran up to them. "I'm Artie, Edward's driver. Is she okay?"

"She will be. Please step back."

Alex placed Nicole on the front seat of his truck, adjusted her messenger bag in her lap and grabbed a wool blanket from the back. He covered her, carefully tucking the blanket around her shoulders.

"Where are you staying?"

"Harbor L-l-…"

"Harbor Lights Inn on Main?"

With a nod she closed her eyes. Alex buckled her seat belt and shut the door.

"Is there anything I can do?" Artie asked.

"Help the officers inside." He rushed around the front of the truck, keeping an eye on the witness.

The witness. That's how he had to think of her or else he'd risk losing his edge. She was the key to finding Edward Lange's killer and Alex couldn't afford to be distracted by her natural beauty or vulnerability.

"Donovan!" Agent Banks called from the front of the house.

"Gotta get her safe!"

"Was it the killer?"

"Don't know."

He jumped into the truck and peeled out of the driveway. "Harbor Lights is five, seven minutes away, tops," he said to comfort her. "I know the owner, Mrs. Cavendish. She can help you change if you're feeling light-headed. We'll go back for your car tomorrow, okay?"

No response.

"Nicole?" He glanced across the front seat. She was unconscious.

With one hand on the steering wheel, he

touched her shoulder. "Nicole, open your eyes."

Her limp body slid onto the seat between them. He took a deep, calming breath. This was not the time to panic, yet the nearest hospital was a forty-five minute drive. He didn't have that kind of time.

She didn't have that kind of time.

He grabbed the radio off the dash. "Dispatch, this is Detective Donovan. I've got a medical emergency, suspected hypothermia, and need a closer alternative than Skagit Valley Hospital, over."

"Waverly Medical Center is open until nine, over."

"Can you let them know I'm coming?"

"Affirmative. ETA?"

"Two, maybe three minutes."

"Copy that."

He stroked Nicole's shoulder, hoping the connection would snap her out of whatever haze she'd sunken into.

"We're stopping by the health center. They'll get you warm and check you out. I'm guessing you've got a concussion," he said.

He gripped the steering wheel tighter at

the thought of the killer stalking her in Edward Lange's backyard. Alex couldn't be sure it was the killer, yet who else would have been out there wandering the property?

He glanced at Nicole and whispered, "What made you run?"

Suddenly he needed to know everything about Nicole Desiree Harris, not only because she was their only witness to a brutal murder, but also because he refused to lose another innocent woman to the tragedy of violence.

He'd make sure Nicole survived the brutal consequence of being in the wrong place at the wrong time.

Nicole opened her eyes and immediately closed them against the bright light. Her head throbbed, keeping a steady beat with her heart.

"Nicole? I'm Doctor Wendell," a female voice said.

A doctor? Wait, where was she? She blinked her eyes open and squinted. A woman's face came into focus, concern creasing her forehead. She looked as if she was in her fifties, with dark hair pulled back into a bun.

Two more people came into view, strangers in scrubs.

Memories of the time her monster father put her in the hospital flooded her entire body. They say your cells hold on to every memory. Nicole would attest to that, as she felt the familiar anxiety skitter across her nerve endings. Even back then no one would listen to her.

No one could protect her.

"Do you remember what happened to you? How you got here?" the doctor asked.

A shudder ran down her spine at the memory. She was cold. Helpless. Struggling to call out for help.

Her vision blurred.

Unable to fight anymore.

The lake pulled her down, swallowing her.

Then she was yanked to the surface by firm hands.

Detective Donovan's blue eyes stared down at her.

"Detective Donovan?" she managed to get out.

"I'm here."

Nic turned her head toward the sound, and that's when she realized her entire body was swaddled in layers of blankets. She actually wasn't cold anymore.

The detective stepped toward her bed. He hadn't changed out of his wet clothes, but gripped a blanket around his shoulders.

"You're still wet," she said.

"We couldn't get him to leave you long enough to change." The doctor pursed her lips.

Alex stepped even closer, his remarkable blue eyes focused and sincere. "You're okay now."

"You promised I would be."

It was the first time that a cop had actually kept his word.

"How do you feel?" he said, placing his hand on the blankets above her right arm. Even through the layers of cotton she could feel the warmth of his touch. How was that possible?

"Okay, I guess," she said. "Am I at the hospital?"

"Medical center."

"I'd like to determine if you fell uncon-scious from the head injury or the hypo-thermia." The doctor pulled out a penlight to examine Nic's eyes. "Okay, without mov-ing your head, follow my fingers."

Nicole followed the doctor's instructions as she tested her vision, hearing, memory and concentration.

"Good," the doctor said. "If symptoms de-velop, like trouble with short-term memory, we can schedule a CT scan."

"I'm hoping to head back to Seattle soon," Nic said.

"Is that where you live?"

Nic nodded.

"When you get there, check in with your primary care provider. Are you feeling light-headed right now?"

"No."

"I don't think it was the bump to the head as much as the hypothermia that knocked you out."

Or, try door number three: emotional trauma of nearly being killed twice in one night.

"I guess you'll need my insurance card."

Nic glanced around the room for her messenger bag.

"I've already handled it," Alex said to the doctor.

"Wait, Detective Donovan—"

"Alex," he corrected Nicole. "I found your insurance card in your wallet and gave them the information. I hope that's okay."

"Yeah, sure, fine."

She found herself shutting down, a little off balance that he'd taken care of her.

Because you're his star witness, that's all.

She leaned back against the pillow and released a quiet sigh.

"Her blood pressure looks good," the doctor said. "Vitals are normal. You're a lucky girl, Nicole. Not everyone knows how to perform CPR properly. When you're ready, Detective Donovan can take you home."

"Thanks."

The word *home* held no meaning for Nicole. It was a nebulous image of something she didn't understand since she'd never experienced the true sense of home. Even her studio apartment on Seattle's north side never quite felt like home. Maybe because she was always ready to pack up and flee in the middle of the night.

The doctor and support staff left the small examining room, but Detective Donovan—Alex—did not. He reached for something on the counter and handed it to her: a coffee cup with a plastic lid.

"This might help," he said.

"Thanks, but I don't drink coffee."

"It's hot chocolate."

"You're kidding."

"Nope. They treat a lot of kids here."

She took the cup and he helped her sit up. This close, she couldn't help but notice well-defined muscles spanning his chest through his soaked shirt.

"You must be freezing," she said.

"I'll dry off later."

"But you could catch cold."

"I'm taking care of you, remember?" he said with a smile.

"Right." She popped off the lid and took a sip of cocoa.

Stepping back, he leaned against the wall and crossed his arms over his chest. "Can I ask you something?"

"Sure."

"Why did you take off like that?"

She ripped her gaze from his assessing blue eyes and studied her cocoa. This was too complicated to explain in three sentences or less.

"You can trust me," he said.

Trust me, Nicole. I'll fix this somehow. But Officer Wheeler didn't fix it, and Nicole spent nine more years dodging fists and protecting her little brother and sister.

"That bad, huh?" Alex said.

"What?" She glanced up.

"By the look on your face I'm guessing you haven't had much luck trusting people."

"Cops especially," she let slip.

"Okay, now *that* deserves an explanation."

Instead, she shut down, wrapping both hands around the cup to warm her fingers.

"You dated a cop," he guessed.

"That would never happen," she muttered.

"Now you've piqued my interest."

This man had saved her life. She owed him an explanation about why she vilified his occupation.

"I depended on cops and they let me down."

"Cops, plural? What kind of sordid past do you have, Miss Harris?"

He was teasing, but the story was far from funny. And not one she necessarily wanted to repeat to a stranger.

"I could always do a little digging of my own," he said. "What would I find? A string of broken-hearted police officers in your wake?"

She pinned him with angry eyes. "My father beat us and every time the cops came to investigate I expected them to help, but they never did. Sure, a few promised they'd get us out of there but did they ever follow through on their promises?" her voice cracked.

Alex touched her shoulder in a comforting gesture. "Take a breath. He can't hurt you anymore."

But she couldn't stop the rant. "He said I could run, but I'd never escape. I'd never be safe. And he was right. Another monster is after me and there's nothing I can do to stop him from trying to kill me, too."

"Don't talk like that. Hey." He tipped her

chin so she had to look into his warm blue eyes. "I'm not going to let anything happen to you."

For a second she was lost in the sincerity of his voice and concerned expression. Then common sense slapped her back to reality. She turned away and studied her cocoa. "I'm ready to go now."

Out of the corner of her eye she could tell he watched her, assessing what to say next, if anything. No wonder he was confused. She was a powder keg, needy one minute and explosive the next, biting his head off when all he did was save her life.

She took a breath and glanced up to apologize, but he'd already opened the door. "Doctor Wendell?" he called into the hallway.

The doctor stepped into the examining room and looked from Alex to Nicole.

"She's ready to go," he said.

Dr. Wendell removed the IV and blankets. "Someone should check on her every few hours."

"I've got it covered," Alex said.

Meaning what? He was going stay close

and protect Nic even though she'd been so incredibly rude to him? If only he hadn't kept pushing her, trying to make light of her past. Yet how could he have known?

"You're all set," the doctor said. "You can return the scrubs tomorrow."

"Thanks," Nic said.

Doctor Wendell left them alone. Nic shifted off the bed and Alex offered his hand for support. She automatically took it and warmth shot up her arm. Incredible. How could his hand be warm when he had to be freezing from the damp clothing?

"You should get scrubs to wear out of here," she suggested.

"I've got extra sweatshirts in the truck. I'll get one for each of us."

She realized they were still holding hands.

And she didn't want to let go.

He must have read fear on her face—fear of depending on someone, fear of being let down again—because he slipped his hand from hers and opened the door.

"Wait," she said.

He hesitated, but didn't turn around.

"Thanks," she said. "And I'm sorry."

"You're welcome, and there's no need to apologize. I have a habit of poking around where I don't belong. I'll try not to let it happen again. Give me a minute to get the sweatshirts."

He stepped out and shut the door with a click.

"I'm an idiot," she whispered. After all, the detective just wanted to help.

Yet her frazzled emotional state was understandable considering what she'd been through tonight. Besides being a witness to murder, she'd nearly drowned.

But she didn't, thanks to Detective Donovan's CPR skills.

She leaned against the bright white wall and closed her eyes. What would happen next? Would federal agents whisk her away and detain her until she remembered something helpful? Would they be able to protect her from the killer who would surely try again?

She had no confidence in the police, but for some reason she trusted Alex. There was something about his deep voice infused with truth and integrity that demanded trust.

Whatever came next, she hoped he'd be a part of it.

Someone knocked on the door. She figured it was Alex.

"Come in."

The door popped open and a tall, bald man with a mustache, wearing a dark suit and aviator sunglasses flashed his badge. "I'm Special Agent Ted Maines with the FBI. You need to come with me."

"But—"

"Please, ma'am. Time is critical. The killer eluded our search of the property. He could be anywhere, even in this medical center." He motioned her out of the room.

She stepped out into the hall and he led her away. Nic kept glancing over her shoulder in search of Alex.

"Where are you going?" Doctor Wendell asked, speed walking to block them.

"FBI." He flashed his badge over his shoulder at the doctor.

"You need to wait for Detective Donovan," the doctor said.

"No, ma'am, I don't." He pulled Nic down

the hall toward the back exit of the medical center.

This is why she hated law enforcement. They didn't respect your feelings or opinions. They just took what they wanted. The agent shoved open the metal door and led her across the parking lot to a waiting SUV.

"Where are we going?"

Would she ever see Alex again?

"Someplace safe."

A shudder raced down her back. There was no such place.

"No." She struggled against his grasp. "Let me go!"

THREE

Talk about stepping into quicksand. Alex blew it in there, questioning Nicole to the point where she'd broken down, confessing her brutal childhood. He was pretty sure she hadn't meant to reveal so much about herself in one breath.

Could Alex have been any more insensitive? Probably not. But he was trying to get her to open up so he could assess how to protect her.

Alex's cell phone vibrated with a call from Chief Roth.

"Hi, Chief," Alex answered.

"I heard you went chest-to-chest with the FBI."

"He was bullying a witness."

"How's she doing?"

"It's been a rough night. She was hiding in the closet when I found her."

"Too traumatized to talk to the Feds?"

"Yes, sir."

"Mark said she gave you the slip?"

"And nearly drowned. She was running from someone. The killer could have still been on the property when we left."

"Not a smart move on his part. What's your current location?"

"Medical center, then Harbor Lights Inn. I have to wake her every few hours due to a mild concussion. Do we still have jurisdiction on this one?"

"Absolutely. The Feds aren't here for the murder case. They've got their own agenda. You did good tonight, Alex."

"I nearly lost the witness."

"But you got her back. Let's focus on PA."

Productive Action was a term the chief had coined to keep his staff focused on solving problems, not feeding them.

"Keep the witness safe. We owe it to Edward to find his killer," Chief Roth said. "I'll call when I know more."

"Yes, sir."

"I'll send a cruiser to sit outside the inn. Never hurts to have someone watching your back."

"Thank you, sir."

Alex shoved the phone into his pocket and pulled a couple of Decker's Lakeside Resort sweatshirts from the truck. His brother never missed an opportunity to promote one of his properties by giving away free sweatshirts with his logo emblazoned across the chest. He'd given Alex a few to hand out to friends, not that Alex had much of a social life since he moved back to Waverly Harbor. At least the sweatshirts would come in handy.

Alex scanned the lot, then pulled off his shirt and undershirt, and yanked the thick cotton sweatshirt over his head. He sensed Nicole needed a moment alone after exposing her past to Alex. He reached into his gym bag for a pair of sweatpants.

"Detective Donovan!" Dr. Wendell waved frantically from the building. "Hurry!"

He slammed the door and took off, panic spiraling in his chest. Had something happened to Nicole? Did she pass out again? Stop breathing?

"What—"

"He claimed he was FBI," she interrupted. "He took her out the back door."

Alex tossed the spare sweatshirt and pants on a chair as he rushed down the hall. What was the agent thinking, dragging her out against her will? Because Alex was pretty sure she wouldn't have gone willingly without checking with him first.

He shoved open the back door and spotted Nicole struggling against a tall, bald man who was trying to shove her into an SUV. Alex had made a promise not to let anything happen to her and he'd blown it. Again.

"Hey!" Alex shouted.

The guy let go of Nicole with such force that she stumbled and lost her balance. Alex tried getting to her before she hit the ground but failed.

The agent used his temporary distraction to jump in the SUV. He peeled out of the parking lot as Alex kneeled beside Nicole. He touched her shoulder but she fought him, swinging her fisted hands against his chest. Or maybe it was somebody else she fought. Her eyes were pinched shut; guttural sounds vibrated against her throat as if she were reliving what just happened.

Or something worse.

My father beat us....

"Nicole, open your eyes," Alex said, removing his hand from her shoulder. Maybe touching her kept her imprisoned in the nightmare. "It's me, Detective Donovan, remember? You're safe. No one's going to hurt you."

Breathing heavy, hands fisted against his chest, she blinked a few times and looked into his eyes with a confused and lost expression. He tried to crack a slight smile to let her know she was okay, that the danger was gone.

That she was safe.

Suddenly she whipped her head around, scanning the parking lot as if remembering what happened. When she finally refocused on Alex, he put up his hands and nodded, silently asking permission to touch her again.

She collapsed against his chest and gripped his sweatshirt with trembling fingers. This time they were not trembling from exposure to the frigid lake, but from the trauma of nearly being taken against her will.

Wrapping his arms around her, he held her close as she coughed and sobbed for a few painfully long minutes. The adrenaline rush alone of what happened to this woman in the past two hours would crack the toughest of men.

"It's okay." He stroked her still damp hair, hoping he sounded more confident than he felt.

An FBI agent just tried to take her out of the medical center against her will? What, to earn gold stars with his boss? Then again, maybe he wasn't FBI.

If not FBI then who was he? If it was the killer how did he know where to find her, and why risk exposing his identity? Nicole and the doctor had seen his face and could give a description.

Alex had another thought: if the guy wanted to silence Nicole why not just kill her in the parking lot?

Something was off here. Seriously off.

"We need to get out of here," he whispered against her ear. "Can you stand?"

"Yeah."

He stood slowly, helping her to her feet. She clung to his sweatshirt as he led her back into the medical center.

"Is she okay?" Dr. Wendell asked.

"I think so." Alex shut the back door to the clinic. "Can you give Nicole another once-over? She may have hit her head on the pavement."

"No, I'm okay." Nicole looked up with pleading eyes. "Can we go? Please?"

He glanced at the doctor.

"It's okay. But watch her."

"I plan to." Alex guided her through the medical center, ignoring the stares of curious staff members and patients. Luckily it was a slow night so there weren't a lot of witnesses to the near abduction, but that wouldn't stop the gossip mill from buzzing.

"Here," Lacy Dunne, the receptionist, handed Alex the spare sweatshirt and pants he'd grabbed from the truck. He didn't even remember dropping them.

"Thanks." He took the sweatshirt and turned to Nicole. "Let's get this on you."

She stared at her hand, gripping his sweatshirt, but didn't unclench her fingers. He sensed that residual fear paralyzed her.

The medical center went oddly quiet and although he knew they had an audience he didn't care. Alex placed his hand over Nicole's and slowly uncurled her death grip.

"You're okay," he assured.

"You said that before," she whispered.

Guilt tore through him. He should have been there for Nicole.

Just like he should have been there for Jessica.

"You're right," he said. "But I'm here now. Nothing's going to happen to you as long as I'm close and I'm not going anywhere. Arms up."

Staring blindly at his chest she raised her arms. He slipped on the sweatshirt and reached around to lift her hair out of the back.

"I can do it," she said.

He lowered his hands and waited until she freed her hair from the sweatshirt. She nodded that she was ready to go just as Dr. Wendell brought over Nicole's messenger bag. "Thanks," Nicole said.

Cupping her elbow he led her out the front of the medical center hoping that he could be true to his word and keep her safe.

The minute Alex and Nicole set foot inside the inn, the nurturing Mrs. Cavendish made them feel welcome, offering food and warm beverages. Since Nicole felt comfortable around the older woman, Alex took the opportunity to slip into the bathroom and change out of his wet jeans into the dry sweatpants. He returned quickly to the kitchen, afraid to leave Nicole's side for long.

Alex suspected Mrs. Cavendish had heard about Nicole's situation, but you couldn't tell by the way the innkeeper was acting. She casually brewed Nicole a cup of decaffeinated tea, served it with a chicken salad sandwich and cookies, and sat at the table chatting with Nicole about the breakfast schedule, the locked door policy and afternoon chocolate tasting on Wednesdays and Saturdays. Mrs. C. was doing her best to act as if Nicole was her average guest yet Alex was sure Chief Roth had called ahead to let her know she had someone special staying at her inn.

Special. Yep, that's the word Alex would use to describe Nicole, and not only because she was a witness to murder. There were many things that made her special, none of which Alex would allow himself to fully appreciate. That would be inappropriate on so many levels.

As Nicole nibbled on her sandwich, Alex leaned against the counter and eyed the window. The Feds would probably show up soon and demand to take her into custody. Their main motive wouldn't be to protect her as much as to get information out of her.

Alex glanced at Nicole, thankful that she seemed comfortable at the inn. It was a warm and welcoming refuge. He'd realized that last year when he'd investigated the break-in of Mrs. C.'s garage that turned out to be kids getting into mischief.

She'd been so grateful to have her boxes of collectibles returned that she started dropping off baked goods at the P.D. every morning. Alex had to politely ask her to stop, joking that he'd already moved his belt over one notch thanks to her culinary talent. She'd backed off, but every week she'd still deliver a tin of muffins or scones to the office. One time she'd sent her niece, Amanda, to make the delivery. That's when Alex figured out he'd shot up to the top of Waverly Harbor's most eligible bachelor list.

Not that he'd encouraged the status. He'd been clear with anyone who'd listen that he wasn't interested in romance. When he'd first returned to town he'd been too busy taking care of Dad to have a social life. After Dad's passing, the pain of losing Jessica resurfaced with a vengeance, still too raw, too fresh for Alex to risk getting involved. He couldn't truly love another woman until he'd healed from his grief.

Nicole yawned. "Excuse me."

"Looks like you could use a week of sleep, young lady," Mrs. C. said.

"I'm sorry. I don't mean to be rude." Nicole bit back another yawn.

"Come on, let's get you upstairs." Alex offered his hand. Nicole pushed back from the table and placed her hand in his.

Her skin was still cold and her fingers felt so delicate against his palm. He nearly picked her up again, but thought better of it.

"Is there anything else you need?" Mrs. C. asked.

"No, just sleep. Thank you for the sandwich and cookies," Nicole said.

As Alex led her through the front room, she gazed longingly at the fireplace.

"You want to relax in here for a while?" he offered. "Warm up?"

She blinked hopeful amber eyes at him. "Could I?"

"Sure."

"That would be great. I just can't seem to get the chill out of my bones."

He knew he should take her statement, but not in her fragile state.

"Let's get you close to the fire." He shifted a thick-cushioned chair in front of the fireplace and grabbed a green-and-yellow afghan.

"How's this?" he said, draping it over her shoulders.

She sat down, folding her legs beneath her. With a sigh, she said, "I may never get up."

"There's no rush."

"I'm sure you have better things to do than play babysitter."

"Not really." He shifted onto the arm of the couch where he had a good view of both Nicole and the street through the front window.

"What about your wife…kids?" she said, staring into the fire.

"No wife, no kids."

"Huh."

"Why, 'huh'?"

"You seem like…never mind."

"I seem like what?" He crossed his arms over his chest in a mock offended gesture and smiled.

She glanced up, but wasn't smiling back. "You seem nice."

The vulnerability in her eyes, in her voice, made him want to look away. But he couldn't. Nor did he know what to do with the compliment or the awkward silence hanging between them.

"I've offended you," she said.

He shrugged, trying to keep it light. "Some guys think the description, 'nice' is the kiss of death."

"Oh, you mean like 'you're nice enough to have as a friend, but nothing more'?"

"Something like that."

She cracked a half smile, gazing into the flames. He lowered his hands toward the fireplace to warm them.

"You know what I don't get?" she said.

"What's that?"

"How you seem to know what I need."

"Excuse me?" He glanced at her.

"Just now, you knew I wanted to sit by the fire."

"You were eyeing it like you needed a sugar fix and it was a hot fudge sundae."

"But you didn't have to set me up here. You paid attention to what I wanted. No one has ever done that for me."

The tormented sound of her voice made him crazy on so many levels.

"Not even your cat?" he joked, trying to cheer her up.

She snapped her attention to him.

"Sorry." He put up his hand. "I'm sure you've noticed that when I don't know what to say to make somebody feel better, I say something stupid."

"How did you know I had a cat?"

He shrugged. "You seem the cat type."

"Meaning what?"

"You have a demanding job managing other people's lives, so I figured a cat is low maintenance. Plus, there's that whole warm-and-cuddly-in-your-lap thing that women like."

"You have a lot of experience with women, do you?" she said with a raised eyebrow.

"I've had my share." He glanced into the fire, not wanting to wander down that dark path. Not tonight, not with her.

She gazed into the fire, as well, and they shared a few minutes of companionable silence. He liked the quiet, the peace it always brought him. Sometimes he'd even drift into silent prayer, surrendering his guilt and remorse, asking God to ease his burden. Alex always felt a little better after prayer. The ache wasn't totally gone, but it was tempered with hope.

As the fire crackled and hissed, Alex realized he'd rarely enjoyed the peace of a quiet moment with a woman. Jessica was always chatting and moving. She wasn't the type to let one unproductive minute slip by. She sometimes criticized Alex for needing time to chill out in front of the TV watching a

Seahawks game. Not that he minded her criticism. She was kinder about it than others had been.

Alex knew he had faults, probably more than most, according to his stepmother, which she drove home on a daily basis growing up.

How did he end up thinking about her? He shook it off.

"So, what's the cat's name?" he asked.

When Nicole didn't answer, he glanced sideways. Her eyes were closed and her cheek pressed against the side cushion of the chair.

He shifted off the arm of the sofa and kneeled beside her. "Nicole?"

Completely out, she looked so content that he didn't want to wake her. Instead, he watched her sleep and thought about the challenges in store for this woman who, it seemed, had already dealt with her share of violence.

"I was going to put another log—"

Alex put up his hand to quiet Mrs. C. She wandered closer to the fire and eyed Nicole, then glanced at Alex with a worried frown.

"She's in trouble, isn't she?"

"Yes, ma'am," he said. "Help me get her to her room?"

Alex scooped Nicole up yet again, and she instinctively wrapped her arms around his neck. He climbed the stairs to the second floor, careful not to jostle her too much and wake her, although he guessed she was completely out from exhaustion.

Mrs. C. motored down the hallway to a room at the end, opened the door and pulled down the covers. Alex shifted Nicole gently into the bed and stepped back as Mrs. C. took off Nicole's shoes and pulled the sheets and comforter across her body. She reached over to turn off a lamp in the corner.

"Leave it on," Alex whispered. "If she wakes up in the middle of the night she'll be disoriented. The light will help her remember where she is."

"There's a sitting room in here," Mrs. C. said, leading him across the room and opening an oak door. "Or would you rather stay in the room with her?"

"The sitting room is great, thanks." He didn't want Nicole waking up with a strange man hovering beside her bed. Even though he'd saved her life more than once, they were technically still strangers.

The sitting room was an ideal spot with a clear view of town and unexpected visitors from its bay windows. A new round of concern arced through him.

"Has anyone called, asking about her?" He pulled back the lace curtain with his forefinger.

"No, why?"

"Do me a favor? If anyone calls asking about Nicole—"

"It's our policy not to share information about our guests with the general public," she interrupted him.

"Good. The fewer people who know she's here the safer she'll be. Is your new security system fully functional?"

"Absolutely. We only have one other guest, Lacy Dunne's cousin, Grace, from Portland. It should be pretty quiet."

Until the Feds showed up.

"There are extra pillows and blankets in the armoire," Mrs. C. whispered as she crossed Nicole's bedroom to the door.

Alex wouldn't need them. There was no way he was going to sleep while Nicole was in his custody.

"What else can I do for you, Alex?" she said, looking up at him with concern in her blue-gray eyes.

"You've done enough. Thank you."

With a nod, she shut the door and Alex flipped the dead bolt. He wandered into the sitting area without glancing at Nicole. Seeing her fatigued body bundled up in the blankets would stir anger in his gut, especially now that he knew what kind of childhood she'd endured. Nicole Harris didn't deserve to be hunted and threatened because she happened to be in the wrong place at the wrong time.

As he studied the harbor lights in the distance, Alex considered moving Nicole to a different location. But for now they would stay put so she could get a good night's sleep and be ready to face the challenges of tomorrow.

Nicole awakened with a start. She gasped, sucked in a shallow breath and whipped her head around, trying to figure out where she was, what just happened. A dream. No, another nightmare.

Shouting. Men shouting.

Only, she wasn't hiding in the closet at Mr. Lange's lake house. She was...

"The inn," she whispered, her voice hoarse, even to her own ears.

Clutching the comforter to her chest she remembered the detective bringing her to the inn, Mrs. Cavendish making her a sandwich and sitting with Alex by the fire. After everything she'd been through she'd somehow managed to enjoy a few minutes of peace in front of the fire with the detective. It had been a surprisingly pleasant moment.

She glanced around the room at the charming knickknacks, antique furniture and lace curtains framing the windows. It was still dark outside so what had awakened her? Was it the anxiety humming through her body from everything that had happened? She seemed to be safe. The detective had said he'd protect her.

Nothing's going to happen to you as long as I'm close, and I'm not going anywhere....

"Detective?" she called out, although her voice didn't carry far. She climbed out of bed, hugging herself against the chill of leaving the down comforter behind, and wandered to an open door adjacent to her room. She flipped on the light. It was a sitting room. Empty.

The rumbling sound of angry voices echoed from the main floor below.

She wouldn't be afraid this time. The rhythmic pounding of footsteps vibrated against the wooden floorboards.

She thought she heard Alex's voice, so she cracked open the door.

He marched toward her room wearing an angry frown that looked so unlike him.

"Donovan!" A tall, broad-shouldered man bounded up the stairs and charged Alex from behind.

He grabbed Alex's arm, spun him around and slugged him in the gut.

Alex hit the floor, gasping for breath.

FOUR

When Alex glanced up, the flash of vulnerability in his eyes shot anger through Nicole's chest. She grabbed a walking stick from the decorative cane stand just inside her room and pointed it at the intruder.

"Get away from him!"

"Put that down!" the guy demanded.

She started swinging, cutting through the air between them, forcing him to back away from Alex who was struggling to stand.

Luckily, she didn't have to make physical contact with the man. The threat of being smacked with a walking stick was enough to make him back off.

"Mrs. Cavendish!" she cried. "Call the police!"

"I *am* the police, lady," the attacker said.

She glanced at Alex, who straightened and

nodded affirmative. "Special Agent Trotter, FBI," Alex confirmed.

She lowered the walking stick and glared at the agent. "But you hit Detective Donovan."

"And you nearly hit me. Which means, I'm taking you in for attempted assault of a federal agent." He took a step toward her.

She raised the walking stick, just as Alex stepped between them.

"You can slug me as many times as you want, but the answer's still the same," Alex said to the agent. "She's in my custody and she stays in my custody."

"She attacked a federal agent."

"You didn't identify yourself to her— as far as she knew, she was defending me against an intruder."

"Aw, isn't that sweet," the agent mocked.

Alex lunged and slammed him against the wall. Heart racing, Nic clutched the walking stick like it was a ninja weapon and she knew how to use it.

The federal officer struggled but Alex pinned him with a forearm to the throat.

"She's not going with you no matter what bogus charges you dream up."

"That's up to our bosses."

Alex stepped back but Nic sensed his body was humming with tension. His fists clenched by his sides, his arm muscles twitched as he glared at the agent.

The front door slammed, and more footsteps pounded up the stairs.

"Our case is bigger than a random murder," Agent Trotter said. "Our previous investigation and Lange's murder are most likely connected, therefore we take priority and the witness should come with me."

Nic darted behind Alex. The agent took a step forward and Alex shoved at Trotter's shoulders.

"Enough!" a gray-haired man ordered, marching up to them. "As police chief of Waverly Harbor, I order you to stand down."

The agent took a step back but still looked determined to take Nicole away.

Mrs. Cavendish came up behind the police chief. The chief narrowed his eyes at Agent Trotter. "My detective's been on high alert protecting a witness to murder who's been threatened multiple times since the crime. I get why Detective Donovan's on edge. What's your excuse?"

The agent glared at the chief.

"Just got off the phone with your supervisor," the chief said. "He's on his way."

Nic stepped out from behind Alex. "He attacked Detective Donovan."

The chief raised an eyebrow at Alex as if surprised that the agent got the upper hand.

"I made the mistake of turning my back to him because I thought he understood the word *no,* that this is our case," Alex said, his voice more calm, his hands no longer clenched. "First you guys try to take her from the medical center, now here at the inn."

"We didn't send anybody to the medical center."

Nicole and Alex shared a look.

"Chief, Dr. Wendell should be able to give you a description of the man claiming to be an FBI agent who tried to take her from the medical center," Alex said.

"Got it."

"She belongs in our custody," Agent Trotter demanded. "You can't protect her. She's been compromised twice since the murder while in your so-called protective custody."

Alex didn't defend himself but she sensed his body stiffen.

"That's not fair," Nic argued. "I ran off the first time."

"You ran off?" the agent questioned. "Why, because you've got something to hide? Have you considered that, Detective Donovan? That you're being played?"

The chief got in Agent Trotter's face. "Get downstairs and wait for your boss. Mrs. C., can we commandeer your kitchen for an hour?"

"Sure thing, Chief. I'll make a pot of coffee." She scurried down the stairs.

The agent didn't move. He glared over the chief's shoulder at Alex. Nic held her breath, afraid the men were going to exchange more blows.

The low buzz of the agent's vibrating cell phone broke the intensity of the standoff.

Agent Trotter ripped the phone off his belt. "Trotter." He turned and took a few steps toward the stairs. "But…yes, sir. I understand." With his back to them, Agent Trotter said, "I'll be in the kitchen."

He disappeared around the corner, and once she was sure he'd gone downstairs, Nic took a relieved breath.

"What a jerk," she said.

Chief Roth extended his hand to Nicole. "Nice to meet you, Miss Harris. I'm Chief Roth. Please know that we're doing everything in our power to protect you."

There was a kindness in his eyes, and she sensed a father-son dynamic between him and Alex.

"Thanks," she said.

"Detective, you stay up here with Miss Harris. I'll deal with the suits."

"Yes, sir."

Alex motioned Nic back into her room without making eye contact. She hesitated, studying him. Was he upset with her for coming to his defense?

"Please," he said, his eyes downcast.

Stepping over the threshold, she wandered to the window, heard the door close and sensed him cross the room to her.

"I would have done it again so you can save the lecture," she said.

"What lecture?"

His voice was close. He was standing right behind her.

"The one where you tell me how I shouldn't have tried to help you," she said.

"Is that what you think is bothering me?"

She snapped her attention to him. "Well, isn't it?"

With a sigh he wrapped a gentle hand around her wrist and raised her hand that still gripped the cane. He tried easing it from her grasp. She didn't let go. She couldn't.

"This is what upsets me," he said in a hushed voice.

"That I used this to defend myself?"

"That you had to defend yourself at all. That's my job. I'm supposed to protect you, yet you were forced to take up a weapon and charge into a potentially dangerous situation."

"It wasn't your fault. Agent Trotter started the fight."

"That's irrelevant." His gaze drifted from her hand, clenching the stick, up to her eyes.

"After everything you've been through you deserve to feel safe, not threatened."

"I feel safe now," she croaked, as a knot formed in her chest.

"Uh-huh," he said, a slight curl to his lips. "Then let go of the cane."

She glanced at her hand clinging to the weapon and willed her fingers to open.

"I...I'm trying."

"Nicole?"

She glanced into his warm blue eyes.

"I'm not going to let anything happen to you."

"You said that before. But you left."

"I'm sorry. I thought you were asleep and I wanted to intercept Trotter before he woke you. I'm here now. I'm not leaving."

"Promise?"

"Yes, ma'am."

His pledge to protect her eased the knot in her chest and she found herself drowning in the sincerity of his eyes. Then she thought she saw something else in the rich blue depths, something she couldn't quite define. So she kept searching for what was behind the curtain, the secret he kept hidden away.

"Look," he said, holding the cane in his hand. "You let go."

He sounded proud, yet all she felt was embarrassment. She was so broken inside that she couldn't let go of a weapon without being coerced. Turning, she hugged herself and glanced out the window.

"Want to try sleeping again?" he offered.

"I doubt that's gonna happen."

"I could read you a story," he joked.

She felt herself smile. "Thanks, but I'm too hyped up. Can we just talk for a little while?"

"Sure."

He motioned to a chair in the corner. She opted to go into the sitting room instead. She slid down the wall and sat on the floor across from the window. Alex reached for the light switch.

"No, leave it off, please?" Nic said.

"Sure, okay." He sat on the floor across the small sitting room and crossed his arms over his chest.

She wasn't sure which made her feel more

at peace: the blanket of stars lighting the sky or the detective's presence.

"So, you want to talk, huh?" he said with a teasing voice.

"What?"

"A guy wants to—" he made quotation marks with his fingers—"'talk,' about as much as a cat likes to be thrown in a tub of water."

"Oscar likes to take showers with me."

"I'm guessing Oscar is your cat."

"Yep."

Leaning against the wall, she realized she was relaxing a little too much. She was the key to solving a grisly murder and when the killer figured that out she'd be next on his list, if she weren't already a target.

Although she'd accepted that she'd never be safe, just sitting here with Detective Donovan gave her hope.

Yeah, false hope.

"Okay, this is your party," Alex said. "What would you like to talk about, Miss Harris?"

"Nic."

"Nic. Huh."

"What?"

"Nic is a good name for a linebacker for a pro football team, not a beautiful woman."

He glanced out the window as if embarrassed that he'd let the compliment slip out.

"Some days I wish I were a linebacker," she said.

Even in the darkened room she could make out his slight smile. How did he do that? How could he enjoy the moment when surrounded by so much chaos?

She fingered the hem of her sweatshirt. "So, what's Decker's?"

"My brother's resort."

"He's not a cop?"

"No, ma'am. He's an entrepreneur."

"Married?"

"He was. It didn't work out."

"And you?"

"Yeah, I work out." He winked.

"I meant—"

"I know what you meant. Married? Almost, not quite."

"It didn't work out?"

"She died a few years ago."

"Oh, I'm sorry."

"Thank you. Every day the pain gets, I don't know, less painful."

"I can't even imagine."

Silence stretched between them. She tried making out his expression but he'd turned his face slightly as if he were lost in the memory, maybe even ashamed. She was curious about how his girlfriend died, but would never be rude enough to ask.

"I was supposed to pick her up," he suddenly offered. "Jessica was volunteering in a rough neighborhood. During the day she could safely take the bus," he said, then hesitated. "Sorry, I don't know why I'm telling you this."

"It's okay."

He sighed. "She was waiting for me outside the community center. It was late, not much foot traffic in the area. Two guys approached her, asked for money and grabbed her purse. She fought back probably figuring I'd pull up any minute."

Nic waited, not wanting to push him, but feeling honored that he'd shared this much.

"She got away and ran into the street to flag down help. Instead, she was hit by a car.

Banged her head against the pavement and died in the ambulance."

"That's horrible."

"Yep. And the odd thing was, no one was charged with her death. Not the guys who attacked her or the driver of the car. No one was responsible. That made me crazy for a long time," he paused. "Until I accepted the fact that her death wasn't their fault. It was mine."

"Don't talk like that."

"I shouldn't be talking at all. But since I just spilled my guts and told you something so personal, it's your turn to share."

"What do you want to know?"

"Why did you become a personal assistant?"

"Well, the pay is decent, the hours are good and…never mind, it's silly."

"What?"

"I like helping people."

"Nothing silly about that. Why do you think I'm a cop?"

"You mean it's not because you love the power trip?"

"Did I look like I was on a power trip when Trotter put me down?"

"No, I guess not."

"You, on the other hand, with your ninja moves waving that stick like you were a black belt." Alex imitated her by motioning with his hands. "I do not want to get on your bad side."

They both chuckled.

"I guess I looked pretty stupid, huh?" she said.

"No," he said, his voice serious. "You looked determined. You're going to need that strength to help you through the court case when we find the killer."

She glanced down at her hands. "Who says I'll be around for the court case?"

"I'm going to protect you, Nicole. The killer's not going to find you."

"That's not what I meant."

"Oh, you mean, if you choose not to be around."

She heard the disappointment in his voice.

"I've fought really hard to survive and build a decent life for myself. I'm not sure I want to sacrifice everything I've worked for by getting involved in this case. After all, I didn't even see the guy who killed Mr. Lange."

"But you heard him."

"I don't know what I heard. I was freaking out." She hugged her knees to her chest.

"Nicole?"

"Yeah?"

"Look at me."

She glanced across the sitting room, and felt his gaze rest upon her.

"What did you think about Edward Lange?" Alex asked.

"You mean as a boss?"

"In general, as a person."

"He was smart and generous. Disorganized, but brilliant. He was dedicated to his work but never took himself too seriously. He knew how to laugh to relieve tension. People thought he was this aloof, uncaring billionaire, but they didn't know he was genuinely kind." She suddenly got choked up as grief washed over her.

"A kind and generous man is dead. Doesn't he deserve justice?"

Of course he did. Nic just wasn't sure she was strong enough to be the one to deliver it.

"Look, I don't mean to overstep my bounds but consider this— As long as you let your fear motivate your decisions, essentially you're letting your father continue to control you."

The mention of her father lit a slow burn in her stomach.

"I'd hate to see fear eat away at you," he said. "If you turn your back on this investigation, on Edward Lange, you may regret it years from now."

She ripped her gaze from his, wanting to say he couldn't possibly understand how she felt, that she'd never allowed herself the luxury of thinking about "years from now." In fact, she felt lucky to survive one week at a time, always on edge, worried that the monster would track her down in Seattle and take out his revenge for losing his family. Nic had been the one to help Beau and Addy escape and leave the violence behind. Once they where safely away she packed up her things, brushed past her drunken father and walked out the door.

His words still haunted her: *you will never be safe.*

And so far, he'd been right.

Yet Detective Donovan accused her of making bad decisions motivated by fear. He simply didn't understand.

"I'm going to try and get some sleep." She stood and padded across the wood floor into the bedroom away from Alex and his accusations. They felt like barbs puncturing her integrity. Was it so wrong to want to protect herself?

"Why don't you go downstairs with the chief," she said, fluffing the pillow on her bed.

"I promised I'd stay with you."

"There are three cops in the house. I'll be fine."

"Nicole—"

"Please." She glanced at him. "Just go."

With a nod, he opened the door. "I'll be close if you need me."

He shut the door with a click.

"I won't," she whispered to herself.

Because she couldn't afford to need anyone.

* * *

After a restless night trying to sleep on the living room sofa at the inn, Alex drove Nicole to the police station the next morning. She hadn't spoken much and he was trying to be respectful of her silence but it was driving him crazy.

He'd blown it, big time, and had no idea how to fix the problem, how to make her trust him again, because that's what he'd destroyed, right? He'd challenged her about running away, yet apparently she perceived it as criticism and judgment. Alex was the last person on earth to pass judgment on another, and he'd never criticize Nicole.

No, he respected her. Which is why the silence was getting to him.

"How did you sleep?" he asked, glancing across the front seat.

She turned and shared a polite smile. His heart did a triple back flip and he suddenly realized the wisdom of handing her off to the Feds.

"Fitfully," she answered. "Nightmares."

"I'm sorry."

"Not your fault."

But it was. He'd been the one to push her, to throw her father in her face when she'd had enough stress for one night.

"Does that happen a lot? Nightmares?" he asked.

"Actually, I haven't had one in a long time."

Which made Alex feel even worse.

"But it wasn't just the nightmares that kept me up," she said. "I had a lot to think about."

"That always makes for a restful sleep," he joked.

A sad smile tugged at the corner of her lips. He ripped his attention back to Main Street, hating that he was the cause of that defeated expression.

Gripping the steering wheel, an internal battle raged on. Maybe he was personalizing this too much, subconsciously trying to make up for Jessica's death by protecting Nicole. Maybe he should, in fact, give bodyguard duties to another officer or federal agent who wasn't haunted by his past.

They pulled up to the police station and she was out of the car before he turned off the engine. He watched her disappear inside, still wearing the green Decker's Resort sweatshirt.

She was probably anxious to ask the chief to hand her over to the Feds, to say that she didn't feel safe in Alex's custody and didn't appreciate his lectures.

He hadn't meant to lecture her but he'd wanted to release her from the controlling fear of the past. As he got out of the truck his phone vibrated. Ripping it off his belt, he recognized his brother's number.

"Quinn, everything okay?" Alex asked.

"I should be asking you that question. I heard Edward Lange was killed last night."

"Yes, unfortunately that's true."

"Word is, either by an ex-lover, or competitor who he drove out of business."

"Are you asking or telling?"

"Neither, just touching base."

"You're not getting any fuel for the gossip fire from me, little brother."

"That's why you think I called," Quinn said, his voice flat.

Somehow Alex had stepped into a hole again.

"Sorry, I'm going on no sleep and haven't had my coffee yet," Alex apologized.

"Whatever. You're obviously okay."

"Quinn—"

"Later."

With a frustrated sigh, Alex shoved the phone back onto his belt and headed for the station. He had to shelve the family drama and stay focused on solving the Edward Lange murder. Truth was, Alex and his little brother communicated as well as two people who spoke completely different languages. Yet now, with Dad gone, Quinn was Alex's only family and he often found himself praying for guidance on how to heal the breach that had grown so wide between them.

Alex knew when it started: when he ran away from the stepmonster to join the army and left Quinn at home to take the emotional hits. Alex took off and never looked back, finished his tour and moved to Denver to become a cop.

He hadn't given much thought to what living with Sophia, also known as the dragon lady, would do to Quinn or their father, who'd been reeled in by the narcissistic former beauty queen.

"And I accused Nicole of running away?" he muttered.

Sleep deprived and off his game, Alex had to get some coffee to clear the cobwebs and help him focus. He opened the station door and was staring at three empty desks. No sign of Nicole, Chief Roth or the secretary.

His heart dropped to his feet. For a second he could barely move, much less think. Then voices drifted from the back cell area and the blood rushed to his head. Feeling like an idiot, he wandered to the coffeepot and poured a cup.

"There he is," said Wendy Livingston, the secretary, as she came into the office. "Chief was wondering where you were."

"I had to take a call."

"The chief's showing Miss Harris our high-tech cell. I think he's hoping that will ease her anxiety a bit."

"Yep, that should do it."

"How are you holding up?" She'd assigned herself as Alex's surrogate mother ever since he moved back and joined the department.

"Tired." He raised his coffee cup. "This should help."

"There's nothing to be afraid of," the chief said, coming around the corner with Nicole. "It's such a high profile case that everybody's scrambling to find the killer."

"Let's hope they don't bump into each other," Wendy muttered.

"Please, have a seat." The chief motioned for Nicole to sit down. "Again, I apologize for the altercation between Agent Trotter and Detective Donovan last night." The chief leaned forward in his chair. "I'd like the two agencies to work together on the case, but the FBI would prefer you go into their protective custody."

"No, thank you," Nicole said.

Great, so she'd decided to run away.

"Your life could be in danger," Chief Roth said.

"I've experienced my share of danger and I've developed excellent instincts to protect myself."

"You can't do it alone," he argued.

"I don't plan to." She glanced over her

shoulder at Alex. "I'd like Detective Donovan to protect me."

Alex put down his coffee. "I'm just one man. You could have a team of agents watching out for you."

"I don't want them. I feel safe with you."

She blinked her amber eyes at Alex and his chest tightened. How was he going to protect this woman when she had this kind of effect on him?

"You're okay with that, right?" she said.

"Sure," he said before he could stop himself.

"The feds are going to fight us," the chief said.

"If they want me to cooperate, they'll need to respect my wishes," she said.

"I agree. The challenge will be finding the killer and keeping you safe at the same time," Chief Roth offered. "Alex is the best detective in the county. It's going to be hard for him to work the case if he's in hiding with you."

"I don't want to hide, either," she said, holding Alex's gaze. "I want to help with the investigation."

"You sure?" Alex said. Last night she was ready to skip town.

"I'm sure."

"Okay, then let's brainstorm a strategy," the chief suggested.

"We could get the word out that Nicole showed up on the scene after the crime was committed and called it in but wasn't a witness," Alex said.

"The techs that processed the scene know that's not true," Chief Roth countered.

"Do they? By the time they got there I was leading her out of the closet. That doesn't mean she was there at the time of the murder. She could have found the body and hid in the closet, fearing the perp was still in the house."

"And if she wasn't there at the time of the shooting she shouldn't be a target," Chief Roth said. "Good strategy."

"But the killer may already know the truth," Nicole said. "He stalked me in the backyard and pretended to be an FBI agent and take me from the medical center."

"I'm not sure either of them were the killer.

He wouldn't risk exposing his identity." Alex rubbed his jaw. "And he didn't hurt you."

The chief leaned back in his chair. "What are you thinking?"

"If she's a witness, a threat, why not just kill her?"

"That's a morbid thought," Wendy said.

Alex glanced at Nicole. "Sorry."

She shrugged. "I've been wondering the same thing."

The station door flew open and a forty-ish woman with blond hair and an angry expression stormed inside. She scanned the room and she pointed an accusing finger at Nicole. "Arrest her!"

FIVE

Alex instinctively took a step toward the woman to block her. "Who are you?"

"Abigail Woods, Edward Lange's sister," she said, her cheeks flushed with anger.

A man stepped into the station behind her. "I'm David Woods, Abigail's husband."

A second man, wearing jeans, a baseball cap and a leather jacket hovered by the door. Must be the Woodses' security.

"Why isn't she in jail?" Abigail accused, glaring at Nicole.

Alex glanced at Nicole, then back at Lange's sister. "Why would she be in jail?"

"Because she killed my brother."

Alex held his ground, keeping Abigail and David Woods a safe distance from Nicole.

"Why are you accusing Miss Harris of murder?" Alex said.

"She has a record for assault. Did she tell you that?"

"No, she didn't mention it." Alex turned to Nicole who studied her fingers clenched tightly in her lap.

"Edward had me run background checks on his employees and suppliers," Abigail said. "I told him about this woman's arrest and you know what he said? He said everyone deserves a second chance, that history doesn't define a person's future. He was so forgiving and trusting and you killed him!" Mrs. Woods shouted.

Nicole's shoulders jerked, but she didn't defend herself.

"Accusations won't help us find the killer," the chief said, walking across the room to Abigail. "Let's talk in the conference room." He glanced at her husband. "Both of you."

David Woods put his arm around his wife and led her past Nicole. Alex didn't miss the hatred in Mrs. Woods's eyes or the shame coloring Nicole's cheeks.

She had a criminal record? How was that possible?

The door closed to the conference room and Alex stepped closer to Nicole. "Nicole?"

She stood and paced to the front window, but didn't offer an explanation.

"I've got some filing to do in the back," Wendy said. "I'll be a few minutes. Can you man the phones?"

"Sure," Alex said, with an appreciative nod. She was giving Nicole privacy to explain herself to Alex.

At least he hoped she was going to explain herself. The heels of Wendy's shoes clapped down the hall and the door to the records room closed.

As Alex studied Nicole, her long hair trailing down to the middle of her back, he wished she'd share the information without him having to push. But as the seconds ticked by he realized he wanted her to confess her past because she trusted him with her secrets.

"Please tell me," he said.

"It was one time. It was my father," she said. "He dropped the charges."

"Why?"

When she turned around Alex read defeat in her eyes.

"It was a game," she started. "His way of proving that he held all the power. He could send me to jail, or release me."

"No, why did you attack him?"

"He had my little brother in a choke hold. I lost it and jumped on my father's back. When that didn't work, I grabbed a broom and started swinging." She looked at Alex with pleading eyes. "Mom died when I was twelve and I took over the mother role for my little sister and brother. It was my job to protect them." Her breath caught and she closed her eyes.

"Go on," he said.

"When Beau was eleven he started acting out, challenging my father. On that day, I truly believed my father was going to kill him. When he finally let him go, Father marched into the kitchen and called the cops. He pressed charges against me. I sat in lockup overnight. The next day he dropped the charges. Beau stopped challenging him. He was afraid the monster would get me locked up for good."

"Why didn't you kids tell the police what was going on?"

"We did tell them! But they didn't do anything. Most of our abuse was psychological and when he beat us he was sure to bruise us in places that weren't exposed. He'd threaten us all the time. He told Beau he was going to take off with my little sister and Beau would never see her again, that Beau would be sent to an orphanage where they'd make him eat fried mud and clean toilets. He'd tell Addy he was going to smother me in my sleep and tell the police she did it. God, the things he used to say to us...."

She shook her head and turned her back to him. Alex sensed she fought back tears. He wished he could take her in his arms and hold her.

He knew the danger of such a gesture. He also knew this woman had suffered enough at the hand of violence. In that moment, he understood why she wanted to remove herself from the murder investigation.

"I never should have scolded you for wanting to run away," Alex said. "I guess that makes me a bully, just like your father."

When she didn't argue he wanted to crawl into a hole. "Where and when did this incident take place?"

"Ten years ago in Spokane, where we grew up."

"I'll track down the case report and speak with the officers involved. We'll explain it to Abigail Woods."

"No." She pinned him with teary eyes. "I don't want people knowing."

"Knowing what? That you defended your brother from an abuser?"

She glanced back outside, but not before Alex recognized shame flooding her cheeks. That particular emotion was a familiar friend of his, as well.

He'd been dealing with years of his own shame, shame over not being there for the people he loved, both Jessica and his family. By running away from his stepmother he'd abandoned his father and brother. He'd always regret not coming home sooner to spend more time with Dad, precious time Alex didn't know was running out.

"What your father did to your family was

not your fault," he said. "There's nothing to be ashamed of."

"I have an arrest record. I was in the house at the time of Mr. Lange's murder. According to Mrs. Woods, that makes me your prime suspect."

"She's devastated about the loss of her brother. Remember how you felt when your dad went after Beau? Abigail Woods just lost her little brother. She probably thought it was her job to protect him, too."

"So you're not going to arrest me? To follow procedure or whatever?"

"I have no grounds to arrest you, nor do I want to. You're our best lead to finding Edward Lange's killer. But after everything you've told me, I understand why you wouldn't want to get involved."

"Alex." She stepped up to him and touched his jacket sleeve. "You were right. Mr. Lange was a good man. I meant it when I told the chief I want to help."

Alex studied her eyes "Are you sure?"

"Yes."

"It won't be easy. We may have to revisit the crime scene."

"I know, but as long as you're there…"

He read trust in her eyes, and he suspected Nicole Harris was not one to trust easily. He suddenly felt the need to draw some boundaries.

"Nicole, we need to keep a healthy perspective here."

"What do you mean?"

"I don't want you becoming too dependent on me."

"Why not? You're the only one who seems to genuinely care about my well-being."

"I'm the lead detective on a murder case. You're my only witness. Let's not get confused."

She narrowed her eyes. "Who's confused? I have something you want. You're not going to let anything happen to me until you solve this murder. Then you'll cast me aside. I get it. I'm not stupid."

She ambled back to the chief's desk and sat down, crossed her arms over her chest and closed her eyes, shutting out the world.

Shutting out Alex.

"Nicole—"

"Anyone call?" Wendy interrupted as she wandered back to her desk.

"No, it's been quiet," he said, not taking his eyes off Nicole.

He'd offended her, maybe even hurt her feelings and that was the last thing he wanted to do. But he had to be clear about their roles in this investigation.

They had a professional relationship. Nothing more.

Then why did he want to kneel beside her and try to explain it again, and in such a way that she wouldn't look so...defeated?

"Do I need to do more filing?" Wendy asked, glancing from Alex to Nicole, back to Alex.

Just then the chief came out of the conference room. He shut the door behind him and eyed Nicole. "They're understandably upset. They want to see the body. I'll take them to the coroner's office. Alex, why don't you take Miss Harris back to the crime scene and see if she can remember anything. And get her official statement."

Nicole automatically stood and walked to the door.

"I'm not sure she's up to it," Alex said.

"*She* is fine," Nicole said, then went outside and shut the door with a click.

Alex couldn't take his eyes off her as she paced to his truck and leaned against it.

"Alex?"

Alex glanced at the chief, who studied him with questions in his eyes.

"I'll check in after I take her to the house," Alex said.

"A federal team will be there until noon. You might want to wait until they're gone before swinging by."

"Yes, sir."

But spending the next three hours with Nicole definitely wasn't a good idea. For so many reasons.

"I thought we were going to Edward's house," Nicole said, as Alex turned his truck onto Lake View Boulevard.

"There's a team there now. I thought it might be better if we waited until the house was empty."

"Why wait? We both want to get this over with as soon as possible."

Which she did because the sooner she helped them solve the case the quicker she could get back to her life. The quicker she could get away from Alex, the detective with the kind voice and caring eyes, a man who acted like he cared about her.

But he didn't. He'd gone out of his way to make that clear.

"The sooner we solve the case, the sooner you'll be safe again," he said.

She clenched her jaw, trying to ignore the sincerity of his voice. She'd been traumatized beyond words last night yet the detective's calm demeanor and warm blue eyes had managed to crack the trauma. No one had ever done that for her before. She'd actually believed she could depend on him, completely.

Their discussion back at the station destroyed that faith with a single sentence: *let's not get confused here.*

So she wouldn't. She'd wear her emotional battle armor and focus on helping the cops, on not getting too personal again by asking about his girlfriend or sharing more details about her tragic family.

"Where are we going?" she pressed.

"One of my brother's resorts. It's peaceful up there. I thought you'd like it."

He was being nice again, caring in a way that could definitely confuse her.

"Just take me back to the house," she said.

"It will be flooded with cops."

"It's fine." She glanced out the side window, watching the evergreen trees whiz by.

"I can tell you're not fine. What's wrong?" he asked.

She resented that he could read her so easily. "Nothing you can fix."

"Maybe not, but I can try."

She wanted to challenge him, to say *why bother?* But she didn't. Just because she'd misinterpreted his caring gestures as personal when he was strictly motivated by his job didn't mean she had to be rude. Detective Donovan was still the most trustworthy person in her life and he was assigned to protect her, so she should bite back her smart retorts and just get through it.

It seemed as if she was always just getting through life.

She leaned back against the headrest and

closed her eyes to discourage more conversation. A professional relationship didn't require discussion, right?

"I didn't get much sleep, either," he offered.

She didn't answer, hoping he'd stop trying to engage her.

A few minutes later the radio clicked on and country music drifted through the car. He couldn't possibly know she preferred country to rock. It was just a coincidence.

The deep male voice sang a tale about a guy seeing a girl for the first time as she ran toward him in the rain. He held the door open, their eyes met and she asked him his name. The male voice mused that if he'd shown up a few minutes later they wouldn't have met that day; they would have missed their chance at love.

It was a song celebrating the mystery of timing, how a few minutes either way can change someone's life forever.

Nic realized if she'd shown up later to the lake house as originally planned she wouldn't have been witness to a murder. Someone else would have called in the crime and she would have been back in Seattle Sunday night.

She also never would have met Detective Donovan, a man who showed her that not all cops were heartless jerks. Sure, she'd been stung when he warned her not to get confused about their relationship—making it clear that it was business, nothing more. She'd been offended that he thought her so weak that she'd become infatuated with him when he was just doing his job.

A part of her had been hurt by his bluntness. A man like Alex would never consider dating a woman like Nicole, not with the baggage she carried on her shoulders like a ten-ton weight.

Dating? How juvenile to even go there. Yet compared to the few men she'd dated in her life, the one sitting next to her seemed the most sincere. He exuded strength of character in a way she'd never seen before. She tried convincing herself that even if they hadn't met in this dire situation she would have been intrigued by Alex Donovan.

But they did meet because of a murder,

and solving the crime was his job, his priority.

He pulled into a parking lot in front of a rustic wood building overlooking the lake. They got out of the car and he motioned to her.

"This is Water's Edge Lodge. Let's see if I can find my little brother, Quinn. I think I upset him this morning."

"You're on a roll," she said under her breath.

"What?"

"Nothing."

He glanced sideways at her.

"I'm tired. Ignore me," she said.

He opened the lodge door and they entered a great room with a vaulted ceiling, log furniture and a roaring fireplace.

"It's beautiful," she said, eyeing the lake through the picture window.

"I'm Alex Donovan," he said to the front desk clerk. "Is my brother on site today?"

"Yes, he is. Let me track him down for you."

Nicole wandered to the window. "What a gorgeous view."

"There's a small beach down at that end, and an indoor pool over there," Alex said while pointing. "Quinn bought the place about four years ago and had it totally remodeled. He's got a great head for business."

"Looks like it."

Alex's phone vibrated on his belt but he hesitated to answer.

"Go on, I'm fine," she said.

He pointed to a patio on the other side of a nearby door. "I'll be right over here."

She nodded and glanced back at the lake. Last night it had nearly swallowed her yet today the sun illuminated the calm surface, giving it a warm peaceful glow.

A young woman stepped up to the window beside Nicole. Wearing black jeans and a denim jacket, the woman looked like she was in her late twenties. She smiled and Nicole returned the smile.

Then the woman narrowed her eyes. "Aren't you Nicole Harris? I'm Cathy Crowell with the International News Service."

Nicole glanced outside for Alex but he'd stepped out of view.

"You were Edward Lange's assistant,

right?" The reporter pulled a tape recorder out of her shoulder bag. "What can you tell me about the murder?"

When Nicole turned to walk away, Cathy blocked her. "Are you a witness? Are there any suspects? Are you a suspect?"

"There you are, sweetheart," a man said, breezing up to Nicole.

He was about Alex's height and build with similar facial features including warm eyes with a tint of green. This must be Quinn, Alex's brother.

"I thought you said to meet in the dining room," he said. "Sorry I'm late."

He kissed her on the cheek and she fought the urge to pull away. She didn't like it when people breached her personal space yet Quinn had come to her rescue so she didn't want to be rude.

"Let's take a walk out front," he motioned with his hand.

"That would be lovely," she said.

He glanced at the reporter whose forehead creased with confusion.

"I'm sorry, do we know you?" he said.

"No. My mistake." She shoved the recorder into her bag.

"Have a nice day." Quinn linked Nicole's arm in his and led her outside.

He leaned close and she thought he was going to kiss her again. Instead, he whispered into her ear, "Keep smiling and don't look behind you."

"Why?"

"More press. They've got a block of rooms. The murder of Edward Lange is big news."

"Thank you for rescuing me."

"My pleasure." He glanced at her and offered a smile that didn't quite reach his eyes. "They'll be watching us, so pretend you're in love with me."

"I don't… I'm sorry, I can't."

He chuckled. "I'm that ugly, huh?"

"You know you're not. I've just…" She hesitated and he quirked an eyebrow. "I've never been in love, not really."

"Oh, sorry." He led her around the corner behind the groundskeeper's shed. He let go of her arm and she realized she felt nothing when Quinn touched her.

As opposed to Alex's touch that flooded her body with warmth.

He reached out to brush a strand of hair off her face. "We've got more in common than you might think," he said with a sad smile.

"What are you doing?" Alex accused as he walked up to them.

Quinn glanced over his shoulder. "Lending a protective hand to a beautiful woman."

"Stop touching her, Quinn." Alex shoved at Quinn's shoulder.

"And you can stop being so dramatic. Where were you, anyway? You left her alone in a lodge full of reporters."

"Why didn't you tell me they were checking in?"

"Why didn't you tell me you were stopping by?" Quinn countered.

"You afraid I'd catch you in a compromising situation?"

"Catch me? What, you think you're my father?"

Their quarrelling was giving her a headache. She instinctively pressed her middle finger and thumb together and tweaked their cheeks.

Alex stopped in midsentence and they both looked at her with the same stunned expression.

"Huh, it still works," she said, proud of herself.

"What did you just do?" Alex said.

"Stopped your bickering. Always worked on Beau and Addy, too."

"Why did you do that?" Quinn asked.

"You're acting like a couple of twelve-year-olds fighting over a new baseball mitt and you're giving me a headache."

"Sorry," Alex said and glared at Quinn.

"Yeah, sorry," Quinn offered.

"I thought we'd find some peace and quiet out here." Alex sighed. "Guess I was wrong."

"Reporters started checking in late last night," Quinn said. "The closest peace and quiet you're going to find is up north at The Sandpiper." Quinn eyed Nicole's Decker's Lodge sweatshirt and shot her a charming smile. "That looks adorable on you."

"Thanks."

"Stop that," Alex said.

"What? Complimenting her?"

"Looking at her like that."

"I give up." Quinn turned and walked away. "Nice meeting you, Nicole."

"Where are you going?" Alex said.

"To work with people who appreciate me, not criticize me for breathing," he called over his shoulder.

"Wait a second."

But he'd disappeared around the corner.

Alex glanced at Nicole. "Sorry you had to see that."

"Don't be. It's nice to know ours wasn't the only dysfunctional family."

"It's just, he's got a way with women."

"What way?"

"He charms them, makes them fall in love then breaks their hearts."

"And you were worried he was going charm me in less than two minutes? Wow, he must be a talented guy."

"He's a frustrating guy." Alex sighed and ran his hand across his jaw. "I guess bringing you out here was a bad idea."

"Let's go back to Edward's house and see if I can remember anything."

"You sure?"

"No, but I can't avoid it forever."

* * *

There were only two forensic techs at the lake house. Nic felt okay until she crossed the threshold into Edward's office. The sight of the bloodstained carpet made her queasy.

"I need the room," Alex said to a tech that was peeling fingerprint tape off the doorknob to the closet.

"Sure." With a nod, the tech left the room.

Alex shut the office door and turned to Nicole.

"Walk me through what happened. That could spark your memory."

Heart pounding, she stepped behind the desk trying to ignore the disheveled room and dust the techs used to find fingerprints. She instinctively wanted to clean everything up. It was in her DNA.

"I was talking to Ruby, my boss, on the phone."

"Where were you standing?"

"Here, behind the desk."

The scene replayed itself in her mind. "I heard the door slam so I hung up." She let her mind drift back to yesterdays's scene.

"What did you hear next?"

"They were arguing."

"Edward?"

"Yes, and another man. I didn't recognize his voice."

"What were they arguing about?"

"I'm not sure. I've never heard Mr. Lange raise his voice like that. Then something slammed into the wall. It frightened me, so..." She walked to the closet and opened the door. Eyeing the stack of boxes she'd used as protection, she fought back the memory. She didn't want to go there again, to feel that terror and vulnerability.

"You're okay." Alex placed a solid hand on her shoulder. "Do you remember what the men were arguing about?"

She wandered inside the closet. "Mr. Lange said it was borderline criminal. The second man said, 'You need to reconsider.' The voices were louder. They'd entered the office, were just outside the closet door." She glanced at Alex but the image of his handsome face started to blur.

"You're doing great," he coached.

"Mr. Lange said nothing would change his

mind, then something slammed against the door."

She backed up, trying to get away from the angry sound of the escalating argument.

"Nicole?" a voice said. Alex. But he sounded far away.

A haze clouded her vision. The men's voices grew louder.

Why are you still here?

Because you haven't called the cops.

The only reason I haven't called the cops is because of my—

The crack of a gunshot slammed against her chest. She gasped for breath and was sucked into an abyss of blackness.

SIX

Alex lunged forward and caught her before she hit the floor. "Nicole?" he said, holding her limp body in his arms.

He carried her out of the closet and marched through the house.

"What happened?" the forensic tech asked.

Alex shook his head and aimed for the back room where he'd taken her last night. He couldn't answer the tech because he couldn't speak past the ball lodged in his throat. He blamed himself for encouraging her to go face-to-face with the fear that had traumatized her last night.

"Can you get me a cup of water?" Alex asked.

"Sure."

Alex laid Nicole on the thick-cushioned sofa and took her pulse. It raced like a speeding train, and her skin was growing paler by the minute. He brushed hair off her face and whispered in a low voice.

"Nicole, it's okay. Please wake up, sweetheart." He hadn't meant for the endearment to slip out but at this point didn't care. If tender words would bring her around then he'd keep talking. "You were so brave. Everything's going to be okay."

The tech rushed into the room and handed Alex a paper cup of water.

"Thanks."

Alex dipped his fingers in the cup and sprinkled water in Nicole's face, once, twice.

With a soft gasp she opened her eyes and her body started to tremble. She glanced around the room. "N-n-n-not again." She sat up and hugged herself, rocking back and forth.

Alex glanced at the tech. "I've got this, thanks."

The guy nodded and left them alone.

"Nicole?" Alex said.

She didn't answer, just continued to rock. Alex shifted onto the couch and pulled her against his chest. He didn't know what else to do.

"Take a deep breath. Everything's okay."

"Why am I here again?" her muffled voice said against his chest.

"You were trying to remember what happened last night and you passed out."

"I'm scared."

"You're safe. I've got you." Alex held her and rocked slightly. As each minute passed, her trembling subsided.

"Mr. Lange was shouting then I heard a muffled pop then screaming and crashing. I think they were fighting over a business decision."

"It sounded like it."

"So I told you what they were saying?"

"You don't remember?"

"The last thing I remember is walking into the closet."

"I'm sorry you had to go through that." He stroked her hair. "It's over now."

"It won't be over until you find the killer."

"Thanks to you we're that much closer." It felt so natural to hold her like this. "I was worried about you."

She suddenly pushed away. "Your witness is fine, detective. What else do you need me to do?"

"That's not what I meant."

She stood and wandered to the window. "I'd offer to go through his office to see what's missing but this was my first time at the lake house so I wouldn't know what to look for. I could search his computer files to see if anything looks odd. That means I'll have to go back in there." She glanced over her shoulder with worry in her eyes.

Alex stood. "FBI took the computer."

"Then I guess my work is done here. I'd appreciate a ride back to the inn." She headed for the door.

Alex caught up to her and touched her arm. "Stop for a second." She was acting too aloof, detached.

"Hey," he said, searching her eyes. She looked past him toward the front door. "You sure you're okay?"

"Stop looking at me like that."

"Like what?"

"Like you really care." She pinned him with angry eyes. "You don't want me to get confused but you hold me and make me feel safe and ask me if I'm okay, like you're genuinely worried about me."

"I am."

"'Let's not get confused here.' Your words, remember? Well, I'm more than a little vulnerable right now and would appreciate you backing off because your compassion feels like you *do* care and I realize this is only a job for you. So, if you wouldn't mind, I'd like to go back to the inn to recover in my room. Alone."

She held his gaze with challenge. He stepped back and she marched to the front door.

Frustration tangled his gut into knots. He hadn't been able to keep a lid on the feelings brewing inside, feelings that crossed the boundary from professional cop to something more intimate.

She'd sensed it, too. Worse, she'd thrown his words back at him, words he'd spoken to set a safe boundary.

Only, how could he expect her to honor the boundary when he kept crossing it? Talk about confused. It seemed as if he was the confused one in this relationship, a relationship that was drifting away from a clearly defined cop-witness dynamic.

He followed her to the truck, wondering how he was going to get his feelings in check when they'd already taken off in their own direction: straight into the heart of Nicole Harris.

Mrs. Cavendish served Nicole a delicious lunch of chicken rice soup and a grilled tomato-and-cheese sandwich. Nicole had eaten as much as she could, but truly wanted to relax and sleep off the trauma of remembering what happened last night.

After sleeping away the afternoon, she got up and went to the window seat. She reflected on what happened at Edward Lange's lake house this morning. It was a good thing she'd remembered what Mr. Lange and his killer said because it could help Alex solve the case.

It wasn't such a good thing that reliving the scene caused her to pass out....

And be carried to safety once again by Detective Alex Donovan. He was her lifeline, a grounding buoy in a sea of violent, choppy waves.

But it was all about the case for him, finding a killer. If that meant forcing Nicole into scary places, well, that's what he'd do.

Nic was so off balance right now that it made sense she'd heard more in Alex's voice than professional concern when he'd said she'd be okay.

Please wake up, sweetheart.

She straightened in the window seat. He'd called her *sweetheart.* She hadn't imagined it, had she? The pleading sound of his voice had lit a fire of determination inside of her, making her fight her way back to consciousness. His brother, Quinn, had called her *sweetheart* and she'd felt nothing but gratitude for rescuing her from reporters.

There was no ignoring the fact that Alex Donovan had a profound effect on her, something she'd never experienced before.

"Probably because he's saved your life a few times," she muttered to herself.

His endearment somehow brought her out of the fog. She'd opened her eyes and was caught by the clarity of his blue eyes, and the cross hanging from a silver chain around his neck. It must have eased its way out of his shirt when he leaned over to whisper into her ear.

Her cell phone rang, jarring her out of the memory. She pulled it out of her messenger bag and smiled when she recognized the caller ID. "Hey, Ruby."

"I'm in shock. I just heard about Edward."

"Yeah, it was horrible."

Nicole settled in on the window seat and spotted Alex speaking to a patrolman down below.

"But you're okay, right?" Ruby asked.

"Yeah, but I'm but pretty shaken up."

"Were you there when it happened?"

"Hiding in the closet."

"Oh, honey…" she said, with sympathy in her voice.

"It looks like I'll be in Waverly Harbor for a couple of days to help with the investigation."

"Isn't that dangerous?"

"Maybe, maybe not. We don't know if the killer knew I was in the closet. At any rate, I'm kind of in police protective custody."

"Kind of?"

"The FBI wants a piece of me, too, but the local cops are fighting to keep me in their custody. The detective who found me in the closet is my shadow, pretty much."

"I'm so sorry."

"Thanks. Mr. Lange's sister showed up at the police station and demanded they lock me up."

"Why on earth—"

"That thing with my father ten years ago, you know…."

"It was justified."

"She didn't know the history. Anyway, I don't think I'll be arrested anytime soon considering they found me cowering in the closet in a state of shock."

"I feel so helpless. What can I do?"

"Could you check on Oscar? Just make sure the dry food bowl is full and he's got enough water?"

"Absolutely."

"That would be a huge load off my mind."

"You just witnessed a murder and you're worried about your cat."

"He's more than just a cat. He's my family."

Oscar had been with her since she'd escaped her father.

"Oh, hey, my other line is ringing," Ruby said. "Can I call you back?"

"Don't worry about it. I'll call you tomorrow."

"Be careful."

"Will do."

Nicole ended the call and considered the fact that her closest family member was a cat. Sad but understandable. She'd drifted away from Beau and Addy, probably because the sight of their big sister brought back such painful memories, memories of Nic shoving them into a closet or hurrying them up the attic steps so Dad wouldn't find them. She couldn't blame them for wanting to avoid reliving the horror.

Due to her traumatic childhood, Nicole didn't open up easily to people. Ruby was her one true friend and it had taken Nic three years to share aspects of her dark past with her.

So basically Nic's inner circle consisted of

one good friend and one frisky cat, which made for a very lonely life.

Yet she hadn't noticed how alone she was until she'd met Detective Donovan. It was like her interaction with him exposed a need she never knew she had: having someone in her life she could totally depend on.

And perhaps, kiss.

She leaned against the wall and sighed, admitting the attraction that hummed between them was stronger than she'd suspected. There was no sense denying it, or the fact it would complicate things, because she was pretty sure kissing a witness was not in his job description.

She glanced outside just as Alex looked up from his conversation with the patrolman. He shot her one of his half smiles meant to comfort her. Her heart skipped a beat and excitement flooded her belly.

"This can't happen." She shifted off the window seat and searched the room for a good book, something to distract her runaway thoughts. She opened the glass bookcase and there, centering a collection of classics, was a Bible.

She stared at it, wishing there was something inside the pages that could give her peace, but she'd given up on God long ago. Where was God when a drunk driver killed her mother? Where was God when Dad came after her, or Beau or Addy?

She shut the glass doors but her gaze lingered on the Bible. A small part of her ached for a connection to God.

She simply couldn't get past the anger, the resentment.

A soft tap on the door interrupted her thoughts.

"Come in," she said.

Alex opened the door and ambled across the room to stand next to her. "Find anything interesting?"

She ripped her gaze from the bookcase and wandered back to the window seat. "Not really."

A few seconds of awkward silence stretched between them.

"So, what's new with the case?" she said.

"We've narrowed down the list of suspects to people Edward worked with, thanks to you." He crossed his arms over his chest and leaned against the wall. "The chief convinced Abigail Woods that you're not a viable suspect."

"How'd he manage that?"

"Shared a little bit of your background."

"I'd asked you not to do that."

"I didn't. Guess he knew someone in the Spokane P.D. and made a call, got the inside story. He also managed to get the Feds to back off a bit."

"He's had a good day."

"Yes, he has. Wish I could say the same. All I managed to do was put you in danger, both at the resort and back at the lake house."

"I thought you said my memories helped you."

"They did. I just haven't had time to pursue the leads, yet."

"Because of your protection detail," she said, her voice flat.

"That's not—"

"Look, I'm better now. Why don't you find someone else to babysit me?"

"I made a commitment to protect you."

"I release you from that promise. Go

ahead, call one of your deputies to take over so you can work the case."

"This morning at the station you said you felt safest with me."

"I'll feel safer once you find the killer and you can't do that if you're here holding my hand."

"Are you sure?"

"Absolutely."

"Nicole?"

She glanced into his eyes, hoping she had the mask of indifference firmly in place.

"What's going on?" he asked.

"I had a reality check. I'm holding you back. It's time I stop being so selfish and let you do your job." She walked to the door, needing to put distance between them. "Mrs. Cavendish is serving lasagna for dinner. Thought I'd head down." She glanced over her shoulder. "Unless there was something else?"

He shook his head, a puzzled expression creasing his brow.

"Okay, then, I'll be downstairs."

She left the room, walking away from Alex's compassionate blue eyes and deep, caring voice. It was better this way. The separation would give them the distance they needed. Alex would be able to focus on solving a murder and Nicole could get her perspective back.

Because she knew, deep in her heart, that depending on someone, especially a cop, would only lead to tragedy.

He wasn't buying Nicole's new attitude and sudden strength, which she wore proudly through dinner like a shield of armor. The conversation consisted of light and meaningless small talk. Mrs. C. commented on the new gift shop opening in town, the questionable future of the old mill property and Mrs. Delmonico adopting her fifth cat.

Nicole seemed absorbed in the conversation. Maybe for her the events of a small town were the perfect distraction to take the edge off her fear.

Because he knew she still had to be afraid.

He'd offered to help with the cleanup but the women herded him to the living room. As he waited by the front window for his replacement, the soft voices of Nicole and Mrs. Cavendish drifted to him from the kitchen.

Nicole's voice sounded relaxed, different than when she'd told him to find a replacement bodyguard. When she'd demanded he focus on finding the killer instead of babysitting her, Nicole's tone had been cool and businesslike. Detached.

Isn't that what he'd wanted, to keep their relationship professional?

What he desperately wanted was to find the killer so she wouldn't be in danger. And now she'd given him the freedom to get to work helping the chief investigate leads instead of watching over Nicole.

Was the tension in his gut warning him not to let her out of his sight? Or maybe it was a reaction to everything that had happened in the past twenty-four hours. Who wouldn't be hesitant to leave her side considering the threats against her life?

"Enough." He needed to put some of his analytical energy into following up on leads.

Did the killer know about Nicole's presence during the shooting? The answer to that question would ease his fear and allow him to step aside and let Mark take over as her protector.

Stop thinking about her safety and focus on the crime.

Alex pulled his computer tablet out of his backpack and opened his email. Lange Industries VP Beverly Lutz was sending over a list of new projects, highlighting the ones Edward had been most involved in and which staff members played lead roles. Once Alex reviewed that list he could narrow down the suspect pool by checking alibis.

He found the email from Beverly Lutz and clicked it open.

"So, did you find someone?" Nicole's sweet voice said.

He glanced up as she padded across the living room.

"I'm working on a list of suspects, yeah."

"I meant to replace you as my bodyguard."

"You're that anxious to get rid of me, huh?" he joked.

Instead of smiling she glanced down at her feet.

Something was definitely off. He knew he

wasn't going to get through her impregnable wall so he tried a different tack.

"Are you up to helping with the case?" he asked.

"Sure."

"I received this email with a list of employees working on various projects. Do you know if Edward was expecting anyone else at the lake house for a work-related meeting?"

"No, I don't think so. Ruby said he needed to get away from the hectic energy of the office so he could strategize."

"Strategize what?"

"I'm not sure."

"What was your role in the strategizing process?"

"Help him stay organized so things wouldn't fall through the cracks. He was brilliant and creative but a tad ADHD."

"I'd like to show you a list of his current projects, just to see if anything jumps out at you."

"Okay, but Ruby was his primary PA."

"I'll let her take a look, as well." He handed her the tablet.

With focused concentration, she ran her finger down the list of projects. She hesitated, pursing her lips slightly.

"What is it?" he asked.

"When I checked his voice mail yesterday, a reporter called about this." She pointed to the Tech-Link project listing. "She wanted a quote about the failure of the project."

"Failure?"

"I don't know what she meant, sorry."

"Do you remember her name?"

"Audrey Ross, with *Tech Worldwide*. It's an online daily news service."

"And Tech-Link?" he asked.

"It's a new security program designed to protect companies against hackers."

Headlights flashed through the window. Alex eyed the police cruiser as it pulled into the driveway.

"Looks like my replacement is here." Alex spotted a concerned frown on Nicole's face just before she turned away. She wandered to the fireplace.

"Mark, Officer Adams, is very capable," Alex reassured. "You'll be safe with him."

"Thank you." She didn't look up.

"I'm just a phone call away." He pulled a business card out of his wallet. "Here, program my number into your phone."

She took his card and did as he'd suggested.

Footsteps pounded up the front porch.

"This *is* what you want, right?" he asked.

"Of course." She glanced at the fireplace. "Nicole—"

A knock interrupted him. Alex opened the door and motioned Officer Adams inside. Alex cast a quick glance down the street. No sign of suspicious activity.

Alex shut the door and made introductions.

"Nicole, this is Officer Mark Adams."

"Ma'am," Mark said.

"Nice to meet you."

Alex couldn't help but notice the tension lines in her face disappear as she aimed a warm smile at Mark, a smile of relief, of gratitude.

"She's not to leave the inn under any circumstances," Alex said. "Check with me if you see anything suspicious. I'm still the lead on this case. The inn has a state-of-the-art security system. Mrs. Cavendish will give you the code. She's back in the kitchen." Alex motioned for Mark to speak with Mrs. C. hoping Alex could get a moment alone with Nicole.

"Yes, sir." Mark started for the kitchen.

"Wait," Nicole said. "I'll go with you. I could use another cup of tea."

Without looking at Alex, she accompanied Mark through the living and dining rooms toward the kitchen. It was like she couldn't get away from Alex fast enough.

He wanted to say something, to apologize for whatever he did that created this breach between them, but she'd disappeared before he could utter a word.

This was the best way to manage the situation. She was in capable hands and secure at the inn.

"Please lock up and punch in the security code after I leave," he called out.

"Will do, Detective!" Mrs. Cavendish responded.

With a final hesitation, Alex grabbed his backpack and left, scanning the street as he walked to his truck. He'd catalogued the cars in the neighborhood earlier when he'd brought Nicole back. Nothing had changed: the vintage blue Chevy was parked on the street, and a scooter sat in a driveway next door.

The chief seemed to think the initial frenzy to get control of Nicole had subsided on the FBI's part, and there hadn't been another kidnapping attempt. She was secure at the inn. He had to let it go.

As he got behind the wheel of his truck he glanced at the house. His eyes caught on the window overlooking the street, the room where he had bared his soul about Jessica to Nicole. In retrospect that had been incredibly unprofessional, yet at the time it had felt incredibly normal.

Another reason to put distance between them. She knew it, too, so she'd pushed him away. She'd realized that he'd crossed the line and she wanted Alex to stay focused on finding a killer instead of being distracted by worrying about her safety.

He pulled away from the inn, struggling to refocus on the case. He should call the *Tech Worldwide* reporter as soon as he got to the station. It wouldn't surprise Alex if the murder were connected to Edward's work. Alex considered how he'd pursue suspects. It shouldn't be too hard to check alibis, especially if he got cooperation from the Seattle P.D. on the other end.

Which made him wonder, why kill Edward Lange in Waverly Harbor? Why not do it in Seattle? Nicole recalled screaming and crashing, which indicated the killer was driven by anger.

This was most likely a crime of passion, not a premeditated hit, which should make the killer that much easier to find. It also meant the killer was more than a bit arrogant if he thought he could casually walk into Edward's home, kill him and walk away without leaving any DNA or trace evidence behind.

The killer was definitely bold, probably with traits of a psychopath. He or she was a person who didn't see the police investigation as a threat.

His phone vibrated and he pressed the speakerphone button. "I'm on my way, Chief."

"Alex," Nicole whispered.

His gut clenched. "Nicole?"

A scuffling sound crackled across the line followed by the slamming of the door. He spun the truck around and raced back. He called dispatch to request backup and turned the corner to the inn.

The entire house was pitch-black.

He whipped to the curb, jumped out of the truck and withdrew his firearm. Approaching the house, he took a deep breath to slow his speeding heartbeat.

A gunshot pierced the night air.

Followed by a woman's scream.

SEVEN

Alex plastered his body against the house next to the back door.

Either Officer Adams had discharged his firearm, or...

No, he would not go there.

Aiming his flashlight through the multi-paned window he spotted Mrs. C. hiding behind the refrigerator with a rolling pin clutched against her chest. He tapped softly on the window and pointed at the door. With a nod, she tiptoed across the kitchen and opened it.

Alex gently guided her out onto the porch.

"The power went out," she whispered, taking quick, shallow breaths. "Nicole was upstairs... Officer Adams went to find her. I heard a gunshot and..."

"Go to the neighbor's."

With an accepting nod, she headed toward the house next door where the downstairs lights were functioning just fine.

He went inside and aimed his flashlight and his gun through the kitchen, into the dining room. Once he knew it was clear, he stepped into the living room where he spotted Mark on the floor.

"Mark." Alex rushed to kneel beside him.

"Somebody tackled me. I'm fine."

"That makes one of us," another male voice gasped.

Alex pointed the flashlight across the room. Edward Lange's brother-in-law, David Woods, was propped up against the door jamb gripping his chest.

"Are you hit?" Alex went to him.

"I'm not shot. But someone nailed me in the chest and ran out the front door."

"What are you doing here?" Alex scanned the room with the flashlight and noticed a walking stick on the floor a few feet away.

"Abigail and I needed a room. We can't stay at the lake house and didn't want to drive back to the city."

Alex turned back to Mark. "What were you shooting at?"

Mark shook his head, his face flushed with embarrassment. "I didn't mean to. It went off when the guy—"

"Is Nicole upstairs?" Alex interrupted.

"Yeah."

Alex aimed the flashlight at the stairs and took them two at a time.

"He never went up there. She's fine," Mark called after him.

Alex wouldn't believe it until he saw Nicole with his own eyes and held her in his arms.

"Nicole?" he called out. "It's Detective Donovan."

"Alex?"

He turned the corner into her room just as she stepped out of the sitting area.

"Are you okay?" he asked.

Arms wrapped around her midsection, she shook her head, indicating that she was not. In three steps he was across the room holding her.

"What happened downstairs?" she asked, her voice muffled against his jacket.

"Someone got into the house, but Officer Adams scared him off."

"I heard a gunshot."

"He discharged his gun." And when Alex came down from the adrenaline rush he was going to let Mark have it for losing control of his weapon.

As she clung to him, he brushed his fingertips across her shoulders trying to ease her fear. The wail of sirens echoed through the window and lights reflected off the walls with the arrival of police and fire responders.

The Feds would probably use this incident as another excuse to take Nicole into custody. Alex couldn't blame them. Tonight his department looked like a bunch of amateurs.

"Was he trying to kill me?" she whispered.

"No," Alex said with truth in his voice. Because he was convinced the killer didn't want her dead as much as he wanted something from her. But what? Figuring that out would help them narrow down the list of suspects.

Voices drifted up the stairs as emergency responders assessed the men's injuries in the living room. Talk about bad timing. David Woods walked into a mess just because he and his wife needed a place to sleep.

Suddenly the lights popped on. A quick scan of the room eased the worry in his chest. Her room looked untouched. The killer didn't get close enough to harm her.

"Do you think he was here?" she whispered, casting a nervous glance over her shoulder.

"It doesn't look like it."

Alex was frustrated beyond words. How did the perp get into the house?

"He could have been here just now," she said. "When I…" she glanced at the sitting room.

"Shh, there's no evidence he was upstairs. Your room wasn't tossed. Why did you come up here, anyway?"

"I needed time alone to think."

"About?"

"Nothing important."

Alex sensed differently.

The pounding of footsteps echoed down the hallway. Alex took a deep breath. If it was the Feds he wasn't sure he'd be able to control his overprotective instincts. There was no way he was going to leave Nicole's side again, no matter what she said or how much the Feds demanded they take her into custody.

Instead, Chief Roth stepped into the doorway with a curious lift of his eyebrow. Alex was holding Nicole much like a man would hold his girlfriend.

"Is she okay?" Chief Roth asked.

"Yes. How's Mark?"

"Bruised, but fine. Embarrassed that he discharged his weapon. Where's Mrs. C.?"

"At the neighbor's."

"I thought the inn had a security system."

"It does. We'll have to find out what went wrong. I don't like the thought of putting Mrs. C. in danger."

"You're assuming it was the killer who cut the lights?"

"It's the most logical explanation. I'm wondering if we should move Nicole," Alex said.

Chief Roth nodded. "Think she'd be better off with the Feds?"

"No." Nicole pushed away from Alex and

eyed the chief. "I don't trust the Feds. I trust Alex."

"This afternoon you'd asked to have someone else assigned to protective duty," the chief said.

"Because I felt I was keeping Alex from doing his job."

"You are the job." Alex smiled down at her, then eyed the chief. "I'm guessing the killer wants something from Nicole, which is why he risked breaking in."

"Or there's another explanation for the lights going out."

"Doubtful," Alex said. "We need to consider an alternate location for Nicole, one that no one knows about."

"I'll leave that up to you. Just keep her safe."

"Yes, sir." Alex nodded at Nicole. "Pack your things."

Nicole had seen safe houses in movies but none of them looked like this. Nibbling on her lower lip she eyed her surroundings: warehouse tall ceilings, rows of metal shelves half-filled with aged wood and high newspaper-covered windows. Alex thought the old mill property on the outskirts of town would be the safest spot to hide out, and she had to trust his instincts, but still…

The place was creepy.

"Nicole?" he said from the office door. "I've got the space heater going in here."

She joined him in the office and sat on a long, vinyl sofa complete with pillows and blankets he'd brought from the inn.

"It's not fancy but we'll be safe here. Look." He turned the computer monitor so she could see the screen. Five images popped up of the four entrances plus the view of the main road leading to the mill.

"Wow, fancy equipment for an abandoned mill," she said.

"That was part of the deal when they sold the property. The development investors had it written into the contract that the mill would continue to provide security until actual development began."

"Aren't we trespassing or something?"

"Quinn is one of the investors. He gave me the code to get in and access the security feed."

"Nice brother."

He turned the computer monitor around and sat behind the desk. "Not that nice, trust me."

"What is it between you two?"

"You mean besides sibling rivalry?" he joked.

"I'm glad you still have a sense of humor."

He glanced at Nicole. "I would completely understand if you'd lost yours."

"I just wanted one good night's sleep without any drama."

He motioned to the sofa. "Go for it."

"Now I'm too hyped up."

"Then how about helping me with a puzzle?"

"Jigsaw? Crossword?"

"It's about the case."

"Right, sorry."

A part of her wished for a normal night with this man, a night where their biggest challenge was figuring out the five letter word for critical human organ.

"Why do you think Edward dismissed the bodyguards for the weekend?" Alex asked.

"Ruby says he does that sometimes.

Maybe because he wasn't planning to leave the compound?"

"Do you have contact information for the person in charge of security?"

"His name is Carl Whittaker. If you've got internet on that computer I could find his number by accessing Edward's contact list."

"Here, use this." Alex pulled his tablet out of his backpack and handed it to her.

She navigated the website to log in to the private network where Edward kept his calendar and contact list. "Wait, this may not work."

"Why's that?"

"The password changes daily." She entered her log in information and tried the pass code Ruby had given her yesterday: *Cedar*. She hit Enter and the files popped up. "Okay, let's see." She scanned his contacts and found Carl Whittaker's email and phone number.

"Here." She handed the tablet back to Alex. When their hands touched warmth crept up her neck to her cheeks. Was she blushing, too? Drat, she definitely needed a good night's sleep.

"I'll give him a call," Alex said, studying the screen.

She stood and wandered to the doorway, glancing at the rows of abandoned wood.

"You okay?" he asked.

She glanced over her shoulder. "Just tired. Go ahead and make your call. At least if you're working on the case I'll feel like we're doing something productive."

With what she hoped was a convincing smile she turned back to studying the warehouse. She didn't want to be a distraction, and if he interpreted her blush as attraction arcing between them that could definitely jolt him off course.

A minute later she listened as he spoke with Carl Whittaker, asking about the absence of bodyguards at the lake house. Nic wondered how long they'd have to hide out here and who else had the code to get in. How safe were they in the abandoned mill?

She rubbed her arms, hoping to ease the chill from her body. In reality, she had a feeling she'd be cold and frightened until the killer was caught, convicted and sent to prison.

Which could be months.

She couldn't live like this for months.

Closing her eyes, she sighed and wondered why this was happening to her. Was she destined to be shadowed by violence her entire life? Was it even possible for Nic to live a normal, happy life with a husband, and possibly children?

She stopped herself from going down that road. Sure, she'd dreamed of living a normal, safe life, but she didn't think too much about having children. Since she hadn't experienced healthy parenting growing up she feared her parenting skills were slim to none. She wouldn't subject an innocent child to bad parenting.

She'd learned to accept her fate.

Until now.

Edward's death exposed the preciousness of life, the fleeting nature of it all. You could be here today and gone tomorrow without warning or reason.

"I don't like that expression," Alex said, walking up behind her.

She didn't notice he'd ended his call.

"What did Mr. Whittaker say?" she asked.

"That the team got an email directive to take the night off and meet Edward at the lake house Saturday morning. Luckily cameras were rolling and he's going to email me the security feed from that night."

"Sounds like he wanted privacy."

"Yes, but why? What was he hiding?"

She glanced up at him. "You think he was into something illegal?"

"No, I'm just stumped as to why he'd give his security team the night off."

"He was nice that way," she said. "He understood that his employees had families, a life outside of working for his company."

"I thought you were only a temp."

"The dozen or so times I filled in I could tell he was very considerate. Not all bosses are like that."

He leaned against the doorjamb and studied her.

She glanced up at the warehouse windows, careful not to look into his eyes. He had an uncanny way of reading her thoughts and her feelings. And right now she could use a hug.

"What's bothering you?" he asked.

"Other than being a witness to a brutal murder and hunted by the killer?" she snapped. "Sorry, I'm tired of feeling scared all the time. It's exhausting. I thought I'd left all that behind after I got away from my father but the murder brought it all back."

"Anxiety?"

"And the fear I'm destined to be a victim of brutality for the rest of my life."

"Hey, don't talk like that."

"Sorry, I know. I sound pathetic."

He reached out and tipped her chin so she had to look into his eyes. "Not pathetic, frightened. You have every right to be. It's okay to feel those feelings and then let them go."

She shrugged and pulled away. "Did you use the word 'feelings'? You're awfully evolved for a guy," she teased.

"Why, thanks, I think." He smiled and the tension in her chest uncoiled a bit.

"I also used to teach a women's self-defense class," he said. "Let me ask you something. Where is the fear coming from?"

"I'm not sure I understand."

"Tell me what it feels like, how it starts.

For instance, when you were in Edward's office, describe what you felt physically that drove you into the closet."

"I heard shouting and something slammed against the wall and..." She clenched her fists by her rib cage. "My whole body tightened up, like it was in survival mode."

"Your body was remembering the past abuse," he said matter-of-factly, without judgment or condemnation.

"I guess."

"And survival mode meant finding a good place to hide."

"I didn't have a choice. My body just took over."

"Which is a good thing. That response saved your life. Don't ever be ashamed of it."

"But I'm tired of running away all the time."

"It doesn't sound like you ran from your father. It sounds like you put yourself between him and your siblings."

"I'm not sure what good it did us."

"Are you kidding? You survived, Nicole. That's remarkable."

"I feel like a coward."

"I could argue with you and try to convince you otherwise but until you feel it in your own heart you will always see yourself that way. What would it take for you *not* to feel like a coward?"

"I guess..." She hesitated. No one had ever asked her that question. "If I didn't have to run. If the abuser actually ran from me."

"Okay." He grabbed a vinyl cushion off the sofa. "I can make that happen by teaching you how to stand up for yourself, thereby forcing the aggressor to back off."

"How are you going to do that?" She eyed the sofa cushion with trepidation.

"By teaching you some moves. A lot of it is about confidence. If you have confidence, you can defend yourself. That's half the battle. Aggressors sense this and more often than not will choose another target. And if they are bold enough to approach you, you'll be ready." He winked. "First, you need to become comfortable hitting things. If a dangerous situation arises you can't hold back. You've gotta give it everything, all the power that petite little frame of yours can muster." He held the cushion between them. "With the heel of your palm, fingers back—" he demonstrated by holding up his right hand "—strike the cushion. Right, left, right. Easy at first, just to get a rhythm."

"I can't."

"Come on, let it fly."

"No."

"You don't want to be afraid anymore, right?"

"No, but—"

"Then fight back, come on, do it." He shoved the vinyl cushion at her and she stepped around him.

But he stepped in front of her.

"Don't! I can't do this!"

He peered around the cushion. "Why not?"

"Because I don't want to be like him."

Alex slowly lowered the cushion. "Defending yourself doesn't mean you're an abuser like your dad."

"I'd be punching, or hitting or whatever you're about to teach me. How is that different than what he did to us?"

"You were innocent children. I'm teaching you to defend yourself against an attacker. There's a big difference."

She planted her hands on her hips and studied the floor.

"Nicole, look at me."

Clenching her jaw, she glanced up.

"I want you to imagine how it would feel to walk down the street and feel confident that no one could hurt you, that you could effectively defend yourself. Can you do that? Can you imagine that feeling in your chest?"

"I guess."

"No guessing. Close your eyes and imagine how it would feel not to be afraid."

With a sigh, she imagined feeling safe in her own skin walking down a public street. A sense of peace flooded her chest.

"Your pulse slows to a normal beat, the muscles in your gut unclench, right?" he said.

"Yes."

"Now open your eyes."

She did and he was inches from her face. "That's because you've released the fear. You can release the fear if you have confidence that you can protect yourself. You protected your brother and sister growing up, but no one protected you. It's time you learned to do that for yourself. You're braver than most people I know. Brave and courageous." He trailed an errant strand of hair off her face and slipped it behind her ear.

The touch was tender and grounding. His admiration meant more to her than she could articulate.

"You think I'm brave?" she said.

"Absolutely. Now, give it your best shot." He smiled and stepped back, waving the cushion as a target. "There's no wrong move here. You're just learning, so mistakes are necessary. And make a lot of noise. Scream, grunt, shout. Sometimes that in and of itself can drive off an attacker."

He thought her brave and wanted to free her from the constant fear humming beneath surface. She struck the cushion, once, twice.

"Harder! Louder!" he encouraged.

"Argh!" She struck again. And again.

"Come on, more!"

"Get away from me!" As she punched the cushion over and over, her heart rate sped up, her muscles fueled with adrenaline, not fear.

"Good job." He lowered the cushion. "Now

I'll teach you my secret weapon—the Donovan Slam."

Alex led her into the warehouse and propped the cushion on a shelf to demonstrate. "Are you a lefty or righty?"

"Righty."

"Okay, then you start with your left hand. Left, right, left." He hit the cushion with his left, right and left heel of his palm. "Then the Slam. Heel of our palm goes up." He demonstrated on the cushion. "So it connects with the nose. Even if you don't break it, it will stun your attacker long enough to get away. Okay, you try."

She fisted her hands then opened them, took a quick breath and repeated what he'd done. Left, right, left, slam.

"It's about the upward motion," he said. "And don't hit too low or his jaw will do serious damage to your hand. Angle it like this." He took her hand and adjusted her wrist so her fingers angled back even more. Holding her wrist he jabbed at the cushion. "See?"

"Yeah." She also felt the warmth of his hand rush all the way to her toes. Who needed a space heater, anyway? The thought made her pull away, but he held her gaze a little longer than necessary.

Alex cleared his throat. "Okay, good. Try it again."

She realized he'd felt it, too, the warmth, the connection. She smiled to herself. At least this wasn't a one-sided attraction.

She wound up and swung, left, right, left, slam.

"Better," he encouraged.

She struck the cushion a few times, feeling more confident and energized than she had in months, maybe even years.

Excitement coursed through her body at the thought of feeling like this instead of drowning in despair. She clung to the confidence as she struck the cushion again. Left, right, left—

The high-pitched crash of breaking glass echoed across the warehouse.

EIGHT

A week ago Nicole would have instinctively ducked. Instead, she peered toward the source of the sound and fisted her hands.

"Get in the office," Alex said, his eyes scanning the warehouse.

He shifted her protectively behind him and withdrew his gun. Once inside the office he went behind the desk and eyed the video feed.

"The building is secure, so don't be frightened," he said.

"I'm not."

He glanced up and eyed her hands, clenched by her sides. "Well, look at you." With a slight smile he refocused on the computer screen.

"Here." He pointed to the monitor. A man

hovered outside the building waving something in his hand.

"I've gotta check it out," he said.

He started for the door and she blocked him. "I'm coming with."

"You're staying here."

"Every time you leave me something bad happens. I'm coming, no arguments."

With a nod of surrender, Alex said, "Stay behind me."

Calming her excited heartbeat, she followed him as he stayed close to the perimeter wall aiming his gun into the dark distance. The long and narrow rows of lumber were subtly lit by outside floodlights reflecting through the windows. There was enough light to navigate down the aisles, but not enough to clearly see what was around the next corner.

Nic took a slow, deep breath and listened intently, hoping a foreign sound could give them a clue as to where the intruder was hiding. That is, if he'd gotten inside.

Another crash reverberated through the mill. Alex shielded her against the wall with his body. They waited for a few seconds, then kept walking.

Feeling as if she needed something with which to defend herself, she grabbed a piece of wood from a stack and held it close. If something happened to Alex she'd be vulnerable and utterly lost. No, she would not think that way.

They walked another twenty feet and he put up his hand in a stop gesture. He toed something on the floor with his boot. Glass.

They glanced up and spotted a broken window.

"Vandals?" she suggested.

"Possible. Let's go." He stepped toward the door and punched in the security code. He glanced over his shoulder. "You sure I can't get you to go back to the office?"

"Nope. I'm with you."

"Okay. Stay—"

"Stay behind you, I know."

Alex pushed down on the metal bar, flung the door open and aimed his firearm left, then right. With a sigh, he holstered his gun. Nic peered around him and spotted a man leaning against a pile of cinder blocks.

Thanks to the outside floodlights she could tell he was in his sixties, with messy gray hair and a partial beard, wearing jeans and a black jacket.

"Warren?" Alex said.

She took a quick breath of relief. Alex knew him, which meant he couldn't be the killer.

Warren glanced at Alex with unfocused, bloodshot eyes. "Phillip, I fought to keep my job, but those selfish, money mongers threw us all on the street."

"Who's Phillip?" Nic whispered.

"His son. Lives in California," he said to Nicole and kneeled beside the disoriented man. "Warren, it's Detective Donovan. What are you doing out here?"

"Standing up for myself. Said my piece. Those bean counters ruined my life."

Alex reached over and picked up a paper bag wrapped snuggly around a bottle.

"I gave them thirty years." Warren glanced at the building with tears in his eyes. "Thirty years."

"I'm sorry, Warren, but this is private

property and you shouldn't be breaking windows."

The older man stood up and wavered. "I'll break five more if it'll make them listen."

Alex grabbed his arm to keep Warren upright. "How did you get here? You didn't drive, did you?"

Just then, a beam of light arced across the property. Nicole put up her hand to shield her eyes. The car stopped and the front door flew open.

A tall man, about Warren's age, jogged over to them. "Sorry, detective. Warren's had a bad week."

"Good thing he's got you as a friend, Vic." Vic and Alex helped an obviously drunken Warren into the car. Vic shut the door and turned to Alex. "We went out for fish and chips with the guys and the next thing I know, he's gone. I had no idea he brought his own bottle with him."

"I'll dispose of the booze," Alex said.

"Phillip's out of the country for a few weeks on business and the anniversary of Madeline's death is next week," Vic said.

"I understand. I'll smooth things over with

the property owners but I need a favor in return."

"Anything."

"Don't tell anyone you saw us here tonight."

Vic eyed Nicole with a raised eyebrow.

"It's not like that," Alex said. "She's in my protective custody."

"Oh, the girl from the Lange murder," Vic said.

"Nicole, this is Victor Pratt, town councilman and volunteer firefighter."

Vic extended his hand and Nicole shook it.

"Nice to meet you," she said.

"Heard about what happened to your boss. I'm very sorry. We all liked Edward very much."

"Thanks."

Vic glanced at Alex. "Protective custody, does that mean…?"

"It means we don't want anyone knowing where she is for the time being. Can you help me with that?"

"Absolutely. My lips are sealed."

Muffled shouting echoed from the car. Nicole glanced at Warren who was waving his fist in a threatening gesture to no one in particular.

"Not sure about Warren, though," Vic offered.

"He probably won't remember much," Alex said. "He's out of it. Thought I was Phillip."

Vic shook his head with regret. "Wish I could do more for him. He's taken a nosedive these past few weeks."

"Tomorrow's Sunday. How about taking him to church?" Alex suggested. "Being around God's love and the love of his neighbors and friends might brighten his outlook on life."

"Good idea. I could make some calls to let folks know he's struggling. That way they'll rally around him."

"Sounds like a plan," Alex said.

"Well, you two have a good night." Vic shook Alex's hand, nodded at Nicole and left with Warren.

Alex motioned to Nicole. "Let's get inside."

As they went back to the building Alex paused by the door and poured out what was left in the liquor bottle. With one last scan of the property, Alex placed his hand at the small of Nicole's back, guided her inside and set the alarm.

They walked silently back to the office, Nicole deep in thought. Tomorrow was Sunday, a day of worship, and she sensed on any other weekend Alex would be at church singing hymns and embracing God's word. She remembered seeing the silver cross dangling from a chain around his neck when she'd regained consciousness in the study. Although God was a complete and utter mystery to Nicole, Alex was a believer and she felt guilty that his job protecting her was keeping him from church.

"You can go tomorrow, if you want," she said, stepping into the office.

"Go where?"

"To church. It's okay if you want to leave me here and attend services."

He glanced at the computer monitor. "I'm not going to leave your side, not until we find the killer."

"Well, I could go with you." She was shocked she'd uttered the words.

His gaze slowly drifted up from the monitor. "I'm honored that you'd do that for me," he said. "But we're trying to keep a low profile. The two of us attending church together in a small town like Waverly Harbor would be like lighting the fuse of a gossip bomb."

"Oh, right. I hadn't thought about that. I don't have a lot of experience with small-town stuff." She collapsed on the vinyl sofa and tipped her head back against the wall.

"Small towns are great but they have their challenges." He glanced at her. "What kind of town did you grow up in?"

"I guess you'd call it a small city. It was pretty anonymous."

"That must have been lonely. It doesn't sound like you were a churchgoing family, but you had school friends, right?"

"Not many. We kept to ourselves—you know, to protect the family secret."

"I wish someone had been there to protect you," he said, in a low, soothing tone.

"Me, too." A few seconds of silence passed. "I wish God had been there for me."

Alex looked up, waiting.

"I prayed to God to help us. I guess I'm just not worthy of God's love."

Alex was suddenly across the room sitting next to her. He took her hand and gave it a gentle squeeze. "Don't say that. We all deserve God's love and forgiveness."

"I wish I could believe that." Tears misted her eyes and she glanced away.

With his forefinger and thumb to her chin Alex guided her to look directly into his eyes. "You are a remarkable, intelligent and kind woman. You are very special, Nicole, and very worthy of God's love."

Time seemed to stand still, like in a dream when everything freezes in midaction. She wasn't sure who moved first but their lips touched with a gentle, warm kiss, a kiss that obliterated all thoughts of danger and insecurity. Her heart silenced the rational side of her brain that whispered this was unwise, unreal.

She surrendered to the soft, tender kiss and slipped deeper into a sense of peace. Peace and, did she dare say, love?

Fear ripped through her, shattering the perfect moment.

She broke the kiss. Avoiding eye contact, she leaned against his chest and scrunched his shirt between her fingers. She could hear his thundering heartbeat against his chest. He felt it, too, the indescribable magic sparked by their kiss.

A kiss that shouldn't have happened.

"Nicole—"

"Don't," she said. "Can we just sit here and not analyze it?"

"Okay." He stroked her hair and she reveled in the sound of his heartbeat.

This was the first time she'd experienced these feelings with a man, intimate, trusting feelings that she ached to explore. But there was a divide between them—his job and her past—and it was ridiculous to think he'd want to be with a woman as damaged as Nicole.

But for tonight, this one night, she'd inhale his woodsy scent and cling to his shirt. She'd revel in his firm embrace and let the steady beat of his heart lull her into a peaceful sleep.

Sometime in the early hours of the morning Alex had awakened and struggled to get his bearings. He glanced down at the mass of red hair and realized Nicole had fallen asleep in his arms, and he'd fallen asleep right along with her.

He'd been that relaxed, holding her, the pressure of her body against his chest grounding him. Within seconds he snapped back to reality, shifted her onto the sofa and covered her with a blanket. As he wandered to the other side of the desk, a knot of panic twisted in his gut. Falling asleep on the job was no way to protect Nicole.

Neither was kissing her.

He spent a few hours going over the case, replaying the scene in his mind and mapping out a game plan. It wasn't easy with guilt and regret taunting his every thought. Nor was it easy to avoid looking at the sleeping beauty bundled up in the white blanket.

With a roll of his neck, he stood and wandered out to the warehouse floor. It was nearly nine. He could start making calls and dig into the backgrounds of people on his short list of suspects.

First he should talk to Nicole about what happened last night, about the kiss.

Can we just sit here and not analyze it?

The ache in her voice had torn at his heart. And that's when the guilt had started: guilt about kissing her, holding her.

And enjoying it so much.

His cell vibrated on his belt. "Donovan," he whispered, not wanting to wake Nicole.

"Everything okay?" the chief asked.

"Yes, sir. Had a little excitement last night. Warren Phelps got drunk and broke a window but we're okay."

"I heard he's been struggling. How's Nicole?"

"Asleep. I gave her a crash course in self-defense. I hope she won't need it but thought it would ease her fear."

"What's the plan today?"

"Make some calls, follow up on leads."

"I know it must be frustrating not to be out there pounding on doors, but you're doing a good thing, son. Nicole Harris is our best lead. Keeping her safe is our priority."

"I agree." Only, not just because she was a witness.

"How about you come to the house for brunch? Gayle is making an apple pancake thingamabob, plus ham and eggs, the usual feast. We can talk about the case and you two can get a hot meal."

"Sounds great."

"Take the back access road. Fewer prying eyes."

"When do you want us over?"

"After church, around eleven."

"See you then." Alex ended the call and took a deep breath. Although he felt safe here at the mill, he couldn't pass up an opportunity to give Nicole a sense of normalcy. A hot cooked meal in the chief's welcoming home could help them both relax.

"Who was on the phone?"

Alex glanced at Nicole, who stood in the doorway with wild waves of auburn hair falling across her shoulders. He bit back a smile at her disheveled, yet endearing appearance.

"What?" She touched her hair. "Oh, right, I should have warned you. I'm scary in the morning, or at least my hair is. Go ahead and laugh, I can take it."

"I'm not laughing." A smile eased across his lips against his will.

She smiled, too, and warmth seemed to float between them.

"We got an invitation to brunch," he said. "The chief's wife is making apple pancakes."

"You mean you'd risk being seen with me in public like this?" She raised an eyebrow.

"Absolutely."

"Don't worry, I'll tame it before we go." Her stomach grumbled. "Wow, didn't know I was that hungry."

"Adrenaline burns a lot of calories."

She turned back to the office and dug in her messenger bag. "How long until we're expected over there?"

"Not until eleven."

She pulled out her brush. "You think it's safe to leave the mill?"

"We're going to the chief's house. Can't think of a safer place."

With a nod and a pensive expression, she started brushing her hair. He considered bringing up the subject of last night, the amazing kiss and trust they shared by falling asleep in each other's arms, but he could tell from her expression that now wasn't the time. Concern creased her forehead and he didn't want to add to it by telling her they needed to keep their distance and not kiss or touch each other again, not like that.

Yeah, and how was he going to do that when it felt so natural to hold her in his arms?

"What's wrong?" she asked, studying him.

"Just tired." He shifted behind the desk and eyed his tablet.

"Did you sleep at all?"

Only when she clung to him, pressing her cheek against his chest. He hadn't slept that well in years. The irony of it was he shouldn't have fallen asleep while she was in his care.

"Yeah, I got a few hours in," he said.

"That's good."

Their conversation died like a flame doused by water. This was the other consequence of the kiss: awkward moments when neither of them knew what to say.

"Thanks, by the way," she said.

"For what?"

"For everything. Coming to my rescue, over and over. The self-defense lesson. Making me feel safe."

She looked at him with wide eyes and paused in mid brushstroke of her long hair. He sensed she was also thanking him for the kiss.

Some part of him wanted to acknowledge it as well but he couldn't admit how much he liked kissing her. It was a distraction he couldn't afford if he was going to keep her safe so she could ultimately find happiness. He was staring to care that much about her.

"You're welcome," he said. "But it is my job."

"Right." Hurt flashed across her eyes.

He wanted to take that last part back, but knew he had to say it to build a barrier between them.

"Nicole, I—"

"Is there a bathroom in this place?" she said, not making eye contact. "Would be a lot easier to tame this mess if I could see what I was doing."

"Sure, just around the corner on the right." He got up to show her the way.

"I can find it," she said. "You stay here and *do your job*." She disappeared around the corner.

He didn't miss the edge of sarcasm in her voice or the sudden chill between them. It was unfortunate, but necessary to keep reminding her that their relationship was based on the business at hand, nothing more.

Maybe, someday, he could actually convince himself of that fact, too.

Brunch was a good choice, he thought as he watched Nicole take a bite of an apple pancake. The tension eased between them while in the company of the chief and his wife. The few hours before they came over were awkward and intense. He'd drawn his boundary with the "it's my job" comment, but she'd taken it to an extreme, barely speaking to him.

After brunch Nicole called her friend Ruby, and grilled her about Edward's current projects, while Alex analyzed employee records for people who were working closely with the computer magnate. Alex had narrowed it down to three potential suspects: Gerry Walker, Lance Anders and Adam Fluke.

He ran the names by Nicole who checked

with Ruby, asking what the employees were like, if any had anger problems or exhibited odd behavior. Nothing unusual stuck out in Ruby's mind. On Monday he'd check with Human Resources to determine if any of the suspects had been off Friday, and he'd have the chief run background checks.

The afternoon passed quickly as Alex and Nicole sat at the cherrywood dining room table and focused on the case. Chief Roth was on the front porch taking a call and Gayle was in the kitchen baking. The scent taunted him, reminding him of what he'd never had growing up and what he'd lost when Jessica died.

The promise of a loving home.

He shifted in his chair, mentally slapping himself back to the present.

Alex eyed the security video Whittaker had sent over. "Edward and his driver pull up at four, then nothing until Deputy Adams and I show up at six thirty. At least, no one came in through the front door."

"What about the back of the house?" Nicole asked.

"That video feed suspiciously malfunctioned. It would help to know why the Feds are interested in him."

Paging through Edward's calendar on her smartphone Nicole offered, "I think he was developing software for government agencies."

"What kind?" Alex asked.

"Not sure, but I know he was trying to dominate the security software market."

Alex considered that piece of information. What better way to access the FBI's confidential files than to create the software that protects them?

Gayle came into the dining room carrying a tray of sandwiches. "I know we had a hearty meal earlier, but that was ages ago. Thought you might be hungry."

Nicole glanced at the wall clock. "I can't believe it's almost six."

"Time for a break," Gayle said, sliding the tray onto the table. A variety of sandwiches bordered a glass bowl of fresh fruit. "You can't think straight with low blood sugar. But save room for cookies."

"Did I hear cookies?" Chief Roth said, coming in from the porch.

"After you eat a sandwich. Iced tea okay with everyone?"

"Sure," Nicole said.

"Sounds good," Alex agreed.

Chief Roth gave his wife a kiss on the cheek and Gayle looked at him with a raised eyebrow. "You still have to eat your sandwich and fruit before you get a cookie, Chief."

"Busted." Chief Roth smiled, then glanced at Nicole. "Just found out that the man on the property the night of the murder was Carter, the groundskeeper's son."

"So I wasn't in any danger? How embarrassing." Nicole leaned back against the chair.

"You did the right thing," Alex said. "You felt threatened and you fled."

"And I panicked, tripped, fell into the lake and almost drowned. Sometimes I think I bring this stuff on myself." Nicole got up and wandered into the kitchen.

Alex focused on reviewing the security feed but he'd lost his concentration. He didn't like how Nicole berated herself and wished he could help her see that her survival instincts were anything but a weakness.

"You've got to admire her strength," Chief Roth said. "If that's what you've been admiring?"

Alex's attention snapped up to the chief. "Sir?"

"I've never seen you this way with a woman, Alex. So attentive, so concerned."

"It's my job."

"Then you deserve a raise." The chief leaned across the table. "We don't always get to choose who we fall for, son. Take Gayle and me, for instance. She was off at school and I'd taken her sister, Kate, out on a few dates. Then Gayle came home for break and, well, it was instant attraction on both our parts."

"I didn't know that."

"It's not something we like to talk about. Her sister, Kate, ended up going away to school and Gayle moved back. Anyway, Gayle and I tried to keep our distance, for her sister's sake. But love is a gift. Turning your back on it just wouldn't be right."

"I'm not—"

"You don't have to explain, Alex. I know what I know. Just try not to let those feelings fog up your instincts. You wouldn't want to get distracted and have her pay the price."

"No, sir, I wouldn't." Alex considered the chief's comment. "I'm that transparent, huh?"

Chief Roth winked. "Like clear glass."

Alex was still processing the chief's comment two hours later when he and Nicole drove back to the mill. The chief and Gayle tried to get them to spend the night but Nicole politely declined. Alex wasn't sure why. Maybe she was uncomfortable in the nurturing, loving home.

"My brain hurts. Is that possible?" Nicole said, rubbing her temples.

"We processed a lot of information today." Alex glanced in the rearview mirror and squinted against the intensity of headlights. The car behind them was following a little too closely.

"At least I feel like I've accomplished something by helping you guys out today."

"Good, I'm glad."

"I couldn't stay at the chief's house. You understand, don't you?"

"I'm not sure." The headlights got brighter, closer.

"I felt bad taking advantage of their hospitality."

"Gayle loves helping people," he offered.

"I know, but—"

The car behind them tapped Alex's bumper and they jerked forward.

"Yikes! What was that?" Nicole turned to look through the back window.

The headlights flashed on and off a few times.

"Is he signaling for you to pull over?" she said. "Maybe he wants to exchange insurance information."

Alex remembered what the chief said about not getting distracted.

The car bumped them again, a little harder. Nicole squeaked and gripped the dashboard.

Dread filled his chest. He was about to lose another woman he cared about. Only this time he'd witness his failure.

Witness Nicole being kidnapped or killed. No, he wouldn't let that happen.

Alex sped up, hoping to put distance between them, but his pursuer floored it and kept pace.

"He must have followed us from the chief's house." Alex took a sharp turn nearly losing control of the car. This was no good. He didn't want to get her killed by trying to outrun their pursuer.

He glanced across the front seat. "When I stop the car, you get behind the wheel and drive back to the chief's house. You remember how to get there, right?"

"Yes, but what are you going to do?"

"Distract him so you can get away."

"No, Alex—"

"Promise me, Nicole," he said, desperation coloring his voice.

"Okay."

"Good, get ready."

Gripping the wheel, he spotted a turn-around up the road. He sped up, hit the break and jerked the wheel left. The truck spun around and stopped. He was facing their pursuer, who'd veered off the road to miss colliding with Alex.

Alex flung open his door and used it as cover as he aimed his gun at the front windshield of the car. "Get out with your hands up!"

The driver gunned the engine. Alex couldn't make out the driver's face. It looked as if he was wearing some kind of mask.

"Nicole, get behind the wheel," he ordered.

She slid over and looked at him with fear in her eyes.

"Floor it and get back to the chief's. Go!"

Alex jumped out from behind the door and flung it shut. He shot at his attacker's front tire and raced toward the bordering trees for cover.

A screech and a crash echoed behind him.

Panic filled his chest.

Did the driver block her escape?

Something nailed him in the side and he stumbled forward, landing chest first on the ground.

He gasped for air.

He heard footsteps pounding against the pavement.

Something slammed against the back of his head and he struggled to focus but his eyes watered against the pain.

And all he could think about was Nicole and the fact that he'd failed again.

NINE

She couldn't do it.

She couldn't abandon Alex.

Nicole spun the wheel and found herself heading back to him. Had she lost her mind? What else could explain her breaking her word? She couldn't defend herself against a murderer and save Alex, could she?

She was about to find out. Swallowing back the fear, she aimed straight for the mystery car. Her heart skipped at the sight of a man, who she assumed to be the driver, standing on the shoulder of the road. He jerked forward, kicking something with his boot.

Not something.

Someone.

Alex.

"No!" She pounded on the horn and hit

the accelerator, hoping the attacker would think her crazy enough to run him down in cold blood.

It must have worked because he took off running. She veered after him, her heart racing into her throat. He'd hurt Alex, kicked him, and who knew what else.

Killed him?

No, she couldn't go there.

Nor could she run a man down with a car. Alex was right: she wasn't her father. She needed to focus on what was important.

On getting to Alex.

She hit the brake, her headlights pinning the back of the attacker as he sprinted into the mass of trees bordering the road. Shoving the car into park she gunned the engine, letting him know she'd be waiting for him if he came out.

Taking a deep breath, she struggled to slow her pulse. She had to get to Alex. Make sure he was okay.

Tears threatened to break free as she shoved the car into Drive and headed to where he lay sprawled on the ground.

Still. Motionless. He'd been hurt trying to protect her.

"He's okay. He's okay. He's okay," she whispered.

And he was the first man she'd felt she could trust with her secrets.

Her shame.

Her life.

She checked the rearview mirror. No sign of the driver. She pulled up alongside Alex and jumped out.

"Alex." She kneeled beside him to feel for a pulse. Strong and steady. That's when she noticed a knot forming on the back of his head. She gently rolled him over. Blood stained his shirt.

He groaned and looked at her with unfocused, confused eyes. "What…what are you doing here?"

"Can you stand up?"

"Yeah."

Keeping an eye on the potential danger hovering in the forest, she helped him up and guided him into the car.

"You're supposed to be—" She slammed the door on his protest and rushed to get behind the wheel. As she opened her car door, she glanced at the other car to get the plate number.

Peeling away from the side of the road, she headed for Waverly Scenic Drive trying to get as far away from their attacker as possible.

"What happened?" she asked. "Were you shot, stabbed, what?"

"What?" he said groggily.

"You're bleeding." She nodded at his shirt.

He looked down, confused. "I don't know." He tipped his head back and closed his eyes.

"Alex?"

When he didn't answer, panic threatened to consume her. "Just calm down," she whispered to herself.

She needed to think clearly. Alex needed medical attention and they needed to stay under the radar. Their attacker must have figured out they were hiding at the old mill, and he'd probably followed them from the chief's house.

Confident she hadn't been followed, she pulled off onto a secluded roadway bordered by tall trees, cut the lights and parked. She reached over and searched Alex's jacket pockets for his phone. Suddenly, he gripped her wrist and his eyes popped open.

"Alex, it's me, Nicole. I need your phone to call for help."

"Nicole?" he repeated.

"Yes. Please release my hand."

"Nicole." He hushed and his fingers relaxed. "Inside…left pocket," he said in a weak voice, closing his eyes.

She reached inside his jacket, ignoring the sticky sensation of blood on her hand, and pulled out his phone. She found his brother's emergency contact number and made the call, glancing in the rearview mirror.

"Donovan," he answered.

"Your brother's in trouble. I need your help," she blurted out.

"Who is this?"

"Nicole. We met yesterday at the resort."

"Where are you?"

"I'll come to you."

An hour later Nicole paced at the foot of a bed as Doctor Monroe examined Alex. She didn't know how Quinn had gotten a doctor to come out on a Sunday night to tend to Alex, but she thanked God his little brother had that kind of influence.

God? She just thanked God? Of course, because even if Nicole wasn't worthy of His love she knew Alex was.

The doctor said the bullet had nicked Alex and it wasn't serious. Then why couldn't she stop trembling inside?

"Now, follow my finger," Dr. Monroe said.

She couldn't bring herself to look at Alex. It would upset her to see her strong, virile protector laying there in such a vulnerable state. A white bandage stretched across his side and dirt smudged his face as he held an ice pack against his head.

Quinn blocked her frantic pace. "Can I talk to you for a minute?" He motioned to the adjoining room.

She glanced in Alex's direction, hesitant to leave.

"We'll be right next door," Quinn assured.

With a nod, she padded across the carpet to the door.

"Nicole?" Alex said. "Where are you going?"

Guilt arced across her chest at the sight of him: bruised and beaten.

Because of her.

"I'll be right next door," she said. "Your brother needs to talk to me."

He eyed Quinn. "Behave."

Quinn shook his head and guided Nicole into the next room. It was another posh guest room, reserved for VIPs at Quinn's new property, the Sandpiper Resort and Spa. She was sure she couldn't afford to stay here on her budget, and appreciated Quinn giving up two of his most expensive rooms for Alex and Nicole.

"What happened tonight?" Quinn asked.

"We were staying at the mill, you know that part, then we went to the chief's for brunch. Hung out there all day and headed back."

"Why didn't you just stay at the chief's?"

"I didn't... I wasn't comfortable with that. We headed back to the mill and a car bumped us from behind, then Alex said he'd distract the driver while I went back to the chief's, so he jumped out of the car and I took off, but I couldn't leave him behind, so

I broke my promise and went back to help and I saw him on the ground, and the guy was kicking him and, and…"

Quinn took a step toward her and she put out her hand. "No, don't. I'm okay."

He dropped his hand by his side. She felt bad for being rude and potentially hurting his feelings, but she didn't like people touching her, especially when she was in a raw, emotional place.

"And you saved him," Quinn said.

"I threatened to run his attacker down but he took off into the forest."

"Did you get a plate number?"

"Yeah, actually I did." She gave Quinn the number.

"I'll call Chief Roth."

She nodded and mustered up a grateful smile. She was glad to have Quinn's help and hoped the attacker would be found, but her primary focus was Alex. "I hate this."

"He's going to be okay," he said in a comforting tone.

Which only made her angrier. "No, I mean I hate that I'm the reason he's lying there, being stitched up and examined by a doctor."

"You're being ridiculous," he said.

"Excuse me?"

He leveled her with intense blue-green eyes. "Did you shoot him or kick him or try to run him down with the car?"

She clenched her jaw and crossed her arms over her chest.

"No, some jerk did that. Maybe the same jerk who killed Edward Lange or even someone who's working for him—the same guy who wanted to hurt you. Yet you raced back into his line of fire to save my brother. Why would you do that?" he questioned, sternly. "Alex told you to leave. Knowing him, he ordered you to leave and not look back."

"I couldn't leave him like that."

"He's survived worse, I'm sure."

"So you would have left him to fight for his life if it was your fault he was in that situation to begin with?"

"If he'd given me an order? Yes."

She shook her head. "Well, I'm not that selfish. I care too much about people."

"Obviously you care a lot about my brother."

"You make it sound like that's a bad thing."

"He wouldn't want you risking your life."

"Tough. I didn't think I had a choice."

"I assume he never told you about his girl-friend who died."

"Actually, he did."

"Then you know he blamed himself for her death. It ripped him apart. Don't do that to him again. I'm not sure he could handle it."

"This is just a job for him. He keeps reminding me of that fact."

"We both know that's not true."

"How do you know anything? I was under the impression the two of you barely talk."

She couldn't believe she was attacking Quinn with such hurtful words, but he'd pushed her too far, exposing the truth: she was falling in love with Alex, and he was possibly falling in love with her.

"It's true," Quinn suddenly said with a hint of melancholy in his voice. "We're not the closest of brothers."

"Quinn, I'm—"

"Don't say you're sorry. It's not your fault. Alex and I are complete opposites and have a hard time understanding each other." He pinned her with sincere eyes. "But that doesn't mean I don't love him or understand how he thinks."

"I was going to apologize for what I said. It was hurtful and rude."

"Because I hit a nerve?" He raised an eyebrow and the left side of his mouth curled in a playful smile.

She guessed it was a cover for pain, so she played along. "I supposed I've developed an attachment to your brother."

"What kind of attachment?" he pressed.

Although she sensed he was teasing, Nicole took a second to consider her feelings for Alex.

The adjoining door cracked open and Alex studied Nicole's expression. He narrowed his eyes at Quinn. "What did you do?"

Quinn shook his head and headed for the door. "I'll call in the plate number. If you guys get hungry, order room service. I've got you booked under an alias." He turned and winked at Alex. "Mr. and Mrs. Charles."

"Quinn—"

"I've got a business to run," he said, cutting Alex off. Quinn shut the door, leaving Alex and Nicole alone.

"He upset you, didn't he?" Alex asked.

"No. I'm upset about what happened to you." She motioned him back into his room. The doctor had left.

Alex ambled to the table by the window.

"What did the doctor say?" she asked.

"Mild concussion, not serious. You know about the stitches. I recall you were in the room when he patched me up."

"Does it hurt?" She sat next to him at the table.

"Not too badly," he said.

But she noticed that he winced when he sat down.

"Maybe you should lay down," she suggested.

Gripping his side, he leaned forward and looked deep into her eyes. "Why did you come back like that?"

"You wouldn't have left me there."

"That's different."

"Right, you wouldn't have left because it's your job, whereas I came back because I care about you and didn't want you to get hurt."

He reached out for her hand and she automatically offered it to him. When he took it, warmth crept up her arm and wrapped around her heart.

"I care about you, too, Nicole, which is why I explicitly asked you to get away, so you'd be safe. I couldn't forgive myself if something happened to you because of my incompetence."

"You couldn't have known we'd be followed from the chief's house. No one even knew we were there."

"Doesn't matter. You've got to promise me you'll put your safety first, before anything else."

"I can't anticipate what I'll do in any given situation, Alex. I wouldn't have believed I was capable of chasing a guy down with a car but I'm stronger than I was a week ago." She squeezed his hand. "Thanks to you."

"Unfortunately, I'm weaker." He tried to pull his hand away, but she held on.

"Weaker?"

"I'm distracted by the chemistry between us."

"So you feel it, too?" she asked.

He glanced down at their hands, rubbing

his thumb across her knuckles. "Of course I do. And because of those feelings I want to protect you but I can't if I'm unable to focus. The thought of the killer getting near you blows my focus to pieces."

"Listen, I'm not the fragile victim you pulled out of the closet. In the past few days you've taught me to be strong and have confidence. That strength has made it possible for me to help you."

"I'm glad you're feeling stronger." He let go of her hand and wandered across the room.

"But?" she prompted.

"In tonight's case I think it was unrealistic confidence." He glanced at her with concern in his eyes. "What if you didn't scare him off? What if he'd pulled you out of the car or shot you? He obviously had a gun."

"Alex—"

"Don't, just listen. I want you to feel strong and unafraid, I do. But I don't want you to act foolishly like you did tonight."

"You're okay, I got a plate number, we're both safe. It doesn't seem foolish to me. What's really going on here?"

He sighed and ran his hand across his jaw. "It's late. Let's get some sleep."

Without waiting for her response he went into her room and she followed. He checked the closet, the bathroom and flipped the dead bolt. As he approached the door connecting their rooms he hesitated. "Don't answer the door, phone, anything, okay?"

"Sure."

"Call me in the morning when you're up and ready to eat. We'll order room service."

He wanted her to call instead of knocking on the door between them.

"Alex?"

"Yup."

"It wasn't your fault."

He eyed her questioningly.

"Jessica."

"Sure it was, but I'm not letting it happen again."

With a nod, he closed the door. A second later she heard the click of a lock.

Shifting onto the edge of the bed, she stared at the door. At least he'd admitted he had feelings for her. With that out in the open they could stop pretending the only reason they were together was because of Edward Lange's murder.

There could be so much more between them than danger and violence. If only they'd met under different circumstances. Yet the constant threat was what inspired Alex to teach her self-defense, leading to a sense of confidence she'd never felt before.

If only she could ease his guilt about his girlfriend. She hated to see him in that kind of pain.

She wasn't sure why, but she opened the nightstand drawer and pulled out the Bible. Gripping it to her chest, she flopped back on the bed.

And for the first time in her adult life she found herself praying to God, not for herself, but for Alex. "Please, God, show me how I can help him."

The next morning Alex awoke early, anxious to get a description of their attacker to Chief Roth. Not that Alex saw much while he was on the ground being kicked like a sack of grain.

But why not just kill him? Alex wondered,

gazing out the window at Waverly Harbor. He took a sip of coffee and replayed last night's scene in his head.

As he ran for cover, he was shot, went down, and was assaulted by the driver. The guy kicked Alex in the ribs, over and over again, without saying a word. He could have put a bullet through Alex's head, but didn't. It was like the driver didn't want to kill Alex—he wanted him to suffer.

Then Nicole showed up, threatening to run the guy over.

The attacker took off but Alex wondered if she'd seen something that could help them identify the man. Obviously not his face since he wore a ski mask, but still she could guess his height, weight and build.

Alex took a few aspirin to ease the pounding in his head and eyed the list of suspects. He checked his phone and spotted the HR director's email. He clicked it open and scanned the information about the three suspects: Gerry Walker worked from 6:00 a.m.—2:30 p.m. on Friday; Adam Fluke had taken that entire week off; and Lance

Anders was seen in the office at 5:00 p.m., so Alex could scratch him off the list.

If only he could head down to Seattle and interview them in person, look into their eyes and read what was going on there. Instead, he called one of the detectives he knew from a task force he'd worked on a few years ago.

"Beck," he answered.

"Detective Beck, it's Detective Donovan from Waverly Harbor."

"Is this about the Lange murder?"

"It is. A few of my suspects are in Seattle and I was wondering if you could follow up, maybe ask them a few questions."

"Sure."

Alex gave him names and home addresses.

"What do you want to know?" Detective Beck asked.

"Ask them how they liked working at Lange Industries and if they can think of anyone who'd want Lange dead."

"The subtext being did *they* want him dead?"

"You got it. If you actually do track them

down I doubt either of them are the killer but they could have valuable information."

"Why wouldn't they be your killer?"

"Our witness has been assaulted since the murder so we think the killer's still here in Waverly Harbor."

"Or he's got a partner."

Alex didn't want to consider that possibility, but couldn't deny it any longer.

"Don't you have her in protective custody?" Detective Beck asked.

"We do."

"Sounds like your killer has an inside track if he's able to get access to your witness."

The thought had occurred to Alex, as well, but he didn't like considering that one of his own team members could be involved in Edward's murder.

"At this point nothing would surprise me," Alex said. "Let me know if you can't locate them and I'll put out a bulletin with the sheriff's office."

"Sounds good. If there's anything else I can do to help you nail this guy let me know. From everything I've heard Lange was a good guy."

"Yes, he was. Thanks."

"I'll be in touch."

Alex ended the call and considered Beck's comment. If someone had a direct line to the police department's next move…

Alex stood and paced his room. No, he couldn't believe it. There was Officer Mark Adams, Officer Greg Preston—who Alex hadn't spoken to since the murder—Wendy and…

Chief Roth.

"Not possible," he muttered to himself.

The chief had been Alex's champion and an inspiration for the entire town of Waverly Harbor. Alex refused to add him to that list. Yet, the killer had found them immediately after they'd left the chief's house.

A soft tap on the door between his and Nicole's room jerked him out of his thoughts. He opened the door. When she smiled up at him he practically forgot what he'd just been thinking about.

"Good morning," she said. "Did you eat?"

"No, I was waiting for you."

"Good, because I ordered for both of us." She motioned him into her room. Three covered plates were set up on the table by the window.

"You already ordered room service?" he asked.

"Yep."

"You shouldn't have done that."

"Don't worry, I got a little of everything. Pancakes, French toast, eggs."

"You shouldn't have opened your door."

"Quinn delivered it."

"All the more reason why you shouldn't have—"

"Stop. Whatever is going on between you and Quinn is your stuff. He and I get along just fine."

"I'm sure you do." Alex wandered to the table and removed a metal cover. His stomach grumbled at the sight of French toast with strawberries and whipped cream.

"I'm actually offended that you're jealous," she said.

He snapped his attention to her. "What?"

"You think I'd fall for Quinn's smooth lines?"

"Women usually do."

"I'm not just any woman in case you hadn't

noticed. I don't trust easily. At least I didn't until I met you." She sat at the table and uncovered a plate. "Pancakes, yum. Wanna split some?" She glanced up and looked at him with curiosity in her eyes. "What's wrong?"

"Trust," he said.

She cocked her head slightly and waited.

"I'm not sure who we can trust anymore," he said.

"Well, you can trust me and your brother, even if you want to tackle him every time you see him." She stabbed her fork into the pancakes and cut them down the middle with a knife.

"No, I mean in my own department," he added.

She glanced up. "What are you saying?"

"How did the driver know where to find us last night? That we'd be heading back to the mill?"

"You're not saying you think the chief had anything to do with it."

"I'm not sure what I'm saying." He sat down and pressed his fingers against his temples.

"I can't see it, Alex. The chief and Gayle are such amazing people."

They sat there for a few seconds in contemplative silence.

His phone rang and he recognized the chief's caller ID. "Hey, Chief," he answered, eyeing Nicole.

"How's it going, Alex?"

"I assume you spoke with my brother?"

"And Doc Monroe. Said the perp kicked the stuffing out of you."

"I just can't figure out how he found us."

"Checked the plate number. The truck was reported stolen yesterday in Mt. Vernon."

"Why doesn't that surprise me?"

"There's more. Edward's driver, Artie Wagner, left a voice mail. Says he's got information but only wants to meet with you. Left his number for you to call him back."

"Okay, hang on." Alex went to the nightstand and pulled out a hotel notepad and pen. Then he noticed the Bible laying open on the bed. A hopeful sign that Nicole was opening her heart to God?

Alex wrote Artie's number down on the notepad.

"I don't want you meeting him alone, Alex. Let me know the details and Officer Adams and I will be backup."

"Thanks. I'll keep you posted."

Alex hung up, unsure that he wanted to include the chief in the rendezvous.

"What is it?" Nicole asked.

"Edward's driver, Artie, wants to meet with me."

"Just you? Not the chief or FBI?"

"Just me. I figured you'd stay here."

"You figured wrong. I go where you go, remember?"

He stood and wandered to the window.

"You'll have backup, right?" she asked.

He glanced over his shoulder at her. "No, I'm doing this alone."

"All the more reason for me to go."

"Why, so you can save me again?" He heard the bitterness in his voice.

"We shouldn't go into dangerous situations alone. We're better as a team."

"But you'd be safer at the resort, in this room."

"You don't know that. Someone could have

seen us check in last night. We're safer when we're together."

"I'm surprised you can say that after what happened last night."

"You're down on yourself because that guy got the jump on you after you sacrificed yourself to protect me? Don't even go there, Alex, not after all the times you've saved me in the past few days. It was about time I returned the favor. Now, eat your breakfast."

He watched her take a bite of her pancakes. Who was this woman? Surely not the same redheaded beauty he'd found shivering in the closet at Edward Lange's lake house.

Something had changed. She'd changed. With straight shoulders and a firm set to her jaw, she exuded a newfound confidence. She said he'd had something to do with that but perhaps she'd grown stronger after reading the Bible. Certain passages always gave Alex a sense of peace when the world seemed to offer nothing but chaos.

He hoped they weren't walking into a mass of chaos when they met with Artie Wagner.

* * *

"What an odd choice," Nicole said as she peered through the trees at the dilapidated church.

Alex scanned the grounds with binoculars. "Why odd?"

"Our meeting is about a murder and he picks an abandoned church?"

Alex lowered the binoculars and glanced at her. "Maybe he's looking for forgiveness."

"You mean he's the killer? No, I would have recognized his voice. I'd met him a few times before."

"Maybe he didn't shoot Edward but he feels indirectly responsible."

"So he blames himself. Seems to be going around." She eyed Alex, but he'd gone back to searching the property for Artie.

"Alex?"

"I got him. He's coming around the back of the church."

"How will he get in?"

"Kids are always sneaking inside. It's not hard." He hooked the binoculars to his belt. "Let's go."

He took Nicole's hand and she absorbed

strength from his grip. Her heart raced with adrenaline as they darted between trees on the outlying property, making their way toward the church.

"I wish you'd stayed back at the resort," he muttered.

"I think I heard that already, like thirty-seven times."

He hesitated, one corner of his mouth lifting into a subtle, crooked smile. "I'm proud of you."

"Why?"

"For getting your sense of humor back." He redirected his attention to the church. "Looks like he's inside."

"What do you think he wants to tell you?"

"Have no idea. He gave me nothing over the phone. Let's—"

A shot rang out across the property. Nicole was slammed to the ground. Wind knocked from her lungs, she couldn't think, couldn't make sense of what just happened, except that Alex's body was pressed firmly against her back.

"Alex," she gasped.

TEN

Nicole struggled to breathe, to get air back into her lungs. She couldn't accept the possibility that Alex had been shot.

"Alex," she gasped and wiggled to free herself but his muscular body pinned her to the ground.

"I'm okay," he whispered against her ear. "We're both okay."

"I thought you were…" She couldn't finish. It hurt too much.

"Shh." He shifted off and rolled her onto her side. "It's okay."

Nicole felt anything but okay. She wrapped her arms around his neck and hugged him tight. With a relieved breath she released him. "You…you threw yourself on top of me?"

"Instinct."

"Having fun?" a male voice said.

Alex whipped out his gun and pointed it at the source of the sound: Quinn.

"I heard a gunshot," Quinn said, stepping out from behind a tree. "But maybe you guys were too busy to notice."

"What are you doing here?" Alex snapped.

"Watching your back."

"You shouldn't be here, Quinn."

Quinn eyed Nicole. "And she should?"

"I'm not having this conversation." Alex stood and helped Nicole to her feet.

The sound of squealing tires echoed across the property. Nicole glanced at the church. In the distance she could make out a pickup truck racing away.

"The shooter?" Quinn asked.

"I'm going in," Alex said. "You two stay here until I give the signal."

Alex took off before Nicole could utter her protest. She did a quick scan of the property and started to move forward but Quinn grabbed her arm. "Uh-uh. He said stay back."

"Funny, I didn't imagine you as a take-orders kind of guy."

"Usually I'm not, but he's my big brother."

She snapped her attention to the church, waiting, hoping for Alex to poke his head out of the back door and wave them over. Although she figured the shooter had probably taken off in the truck, she still didn't like the idea of Alex going into a potentially dangerous situation alone.

"He's a good cop," Quinn said. "He'll be fine."

"You obviously didn't think so or you wouldn't have followed us out here."

"Ah, that's why he likes you. You're feisty."

She barely heard him, she was so focused on the back door of the church.

"You probably see an honorable Mr. Do Good in my brother," Quinn continued. "Every girl's dream guy."

She guessed he was trying to engage her to distract her from the worry they both felt as the seconds ticked by.

"Where is he?" she whispered. "He's got twenty seconds and then I'm—"

Alex waved them over from the back of the church. She jogged across the property, Quinn right beside her.

With a worried expression creasing his forehead, Alex hurried them inside.

"What happened?" She stopped short at the sight of a white drop cloth over what appeared to be a body on the floor. "Is that...?"

"Artie Wagner. Dead," Alex said. "I just called it in. The chief read me the riot act."

"Because you were doing your job?" Nicole said.

"Because he was playing Lone Ranger," Quinn explained.

"Do I look alone, Quinn? The two of you are standing right here, which is actually worse since it could have been one of you lying on the floor in a pool of blood."

"Alex," Quinn said in a chastising tone, like he thought the graphic description would upset Nicole.

"What? Artie was shot to death and is bleeding out on the floor right in front of us. And neither of you should be here."

"It's not your fault," Quinn said.

The room went strangely silent. Alex clenched his jaw and stared past them out the window. Nicole hadn't seen this side of Alex, so raw, so tortured. She wished she knew what to say but didn't want to upset him further by saying the wrong thing.

"I should have had backup. They would have caught the guy as he fled the scene."

"Artie may not have met you if you'd brought backup," Nicole offered, wanting desperately to say something to ease his pain.

"And now he's dead because of our meeting."

"Artie should have met you at the station where he'd be surrounded by cops," Quinn said. "But he didn't, which means he wasn't comfortable around cops, so he must have been dirty."

Alex snapped his attention to his brother. "So, what? He deserved to die?"

Quinn shrugged as he eyed the body. "We all get what we deserve."

Alex grabbed Quinn by the shoulders and slammed him up against the church wall. "Yeah, Quinn? And what do I deserve, huh?"

Nicole could feel the anger floating off Alex but it didn't frighten her. She understood his anger was a normal reaction to a bad situation.

"I wasn't talking about you," Quinn said, calmly.

"Well, I am, so say it. Tell me what a loser brother I was for enlisting and leaving you behind to be tortured by the dragon lady."

Quinn stared at Alex with a passive, almost detached expression. Nicole would give anything to know who the dragon lady was and what she'd done to create such angst between the brothers.

The wail of sirens echoed through the windows. Alex released his brother and strode across the church. He paused at the door. His shoulders rose and fell with a deep, contemplative breath.

"I'm sorry." He walked out of the church.

Nicole snapped her attention to Quinn who hadn't moved from his position against the wall.

"Who's the dragon lady?" she asked.

Her voice seemed to jerk him out of his trance. He relaxed his shoulders and ran his hand through thick, dark hair. "Our stepmother. Not the cookie-baking type."

"She was abusive?"

"Not physically."

Which meant she'd emotionally abused Alex and Quinn.

"How old were you when Alex left for the service?" she asked.

"Old enough. Twelve." He motioned for her to join him outside. "I didn't need to be protected."

She suspected he said the words more to convince himself than Nicole. He held the door open and she went outside.

"Thanks," she said.

"Actually, I should be the one thanking you," he said.

"Me? Why?"

He gazed across the property at Alex, who was waving emergency vehicles toward the church. "For whatever you're doing to my brother. He's actually talking about it, which is good. At least that's what my ex-wife used to say. She was a counselor and kept trying to get me to open up, said it was good for the soul."

"But you never did? Open up I mean?"

"It's done. Why talk about it?"

"Yet you're glad Alex blurted out that stuff about your stepmother."

"It's good for him, not me."

"Oh, okay." She cracked a knowing smile.

Alex approached them. "The chief wants to talk to you," he said in a stern tone. Was he upset because he'd seen her smile at his brother? No, she chided herself, he was absorbed in the case and frustrated that someone killed Artie.

Chief Roth got out of a squad car along with Agent Trotter from the other night at the inn. Not good. She surely didn't want to be taken into Trotter's custody.

The chief planted his hands on his hips and glared at Alex. "You don't call me for backup and you bring along two civilians?"

"It's my fault," Nicole said. "I won't let him go anywhere without me. He's the only one who can protect me."

Agent Trotter snorted in disbelief.

"Detective Donovan reported a dead body in the church," the chief said to Nicole. "That's not very good protection."

"Well, *I'm* not dead."

The four men looked at her as if she'd lost her mind.

"And what about little brother, here?" The chief motioned to Quinn.

"Alex didn't know I was following them," Quinn offered. "I tracked the GPS on his cell phone."

"Aren't you clever? Maybe you should be the detective." The chief eyed Alex. "Detective Donovan should have seen you following him. He is usually very observant."

"Hey, he's recovering from being beaten up last night," Nicole defended.

Alex shook his head slightly, indicating he didn't want her help.

A brown sedan screeched to a stop and David Woods jumped out. "What happened?"

"What are you doing here, Mr. Woods?" the chief asked.

"Artie Wagner sent me an email asking to meet with him at two."

"Please go back to your car and I'll speak with you in a minute," the chief said.

"He said he had information about who killed Edward. Finding her brother's killer is the only thing I can do for Abigail."

"I'm sorry, sir, but Artie Wagner is dead," the chief said.

David glanced at the church. "Oh."

"Please, wait in your car," the chief said.

With an absent nod David Woods walked away.

"This case is a mess. You've got two dead bodies, and you're no closer to narrowing down your list of suspects," Agent Trotter said. "Chief, I have to insist—"

"Detective Donovan, I'm placing you on temporary leave," the chief said.

"What?" Alex's eyes widened as if he'd been slugged in the gut.

"Come on, Chief," Quinn argued.

Nicole noticed Agent Trotter eyeing her like a steak fresh off the grill. He wanted her in his custody and today's events might get him his wish.

"Then I'll be taking Miss Harris with me." Trotter moved forward and Alex automatically stepped between them.

"You're on leave, detective," Trotter said.

"But Miss Harris is still in our protective custody," the chief said. "You're welcome to interview her any time."

"It's obvious that your small department is incapable of protecting the witness. Since she's been in your custody she's had her life threatened multiple times and was brought to the scene of a suspect interview turned murder. How is that competent protection?" Trotter looked at Nicole. "Ma'am, you have to see how dangerous it is to stay in Waverly Harbor police custody. Please, come with me. We'll put you up in a safe house."

"Agent Trotter, all you care about is uncovering information to prove Edward Lange was a criminal," Nicole accused. "I don't think you're serious about finding his killer and I know you don't care about me and what I want."

"But Detective Donovan does? Lady, you've got a bad case of transference. Your emotions are driving your decisions and they're going to get you killed. Donovan doesn't care about you any more than I do, right, detective?"

Nicole eyed Alex. A war raged on behind those blue eyes. If he said he cared about her he could be disciplined and lose his job for being unprofessional; if he said he didn't care he knew it would crush Nicole.

"Chief, do you need my statement about today?" she said, changing the subject.

"Yes, I'll have an officer take you to the station where you'll be safe."

"Alex can take me." She took a step toward Alex, but the hard look on his face made her hesitate.

"Quinn, take her to the station." Alex turned and walked toward his car.

She wasn't going to call after him, not in front of his boss and the FBI agent. She'd wait until she got back to the resort, then she'd persistently knock until he opened the door between them and talked to her. That is, if he returned to the resort.

"You're not seriously going to let her go in this guy's custody," Trotter said as he nodded at Quinn. "I've done background. He's a playboy businessman."

"Guess you missed the part where I did a tour in Iraq and a few years as a Black Ops agent," Quinn said.

"She can ride with Quinn if she prefers,"

the chief said. "I'll have an officer follow them."

Quinn offered his arm to Nicole and she took it, holding her breath, waiting for Agent Trotter to come after her. She made conversation to distract herself.

"Black Ops?" she said to Quinn.

"My wild youth. Have I got stories…"

"I'll bet."

As they passed Alex she tried to make eye contact to let him know she was here for him, whatever he needed, but Alex was focused on his cell phone.

Quinn opened the passenger door of his shiny Lexus and placed his hand on her shoulder. When she looked up she was surprised by the odd expression on his face. The desperation in his eyes made him seem young and vulnerable.

"He'll be okay," he said.

She heard the second part of his thought even though he didn't say it: *he has to be.*

She slid into the front seat and he shut the door. At that moment she realized how much Quinn loved and worried about his brother.

Although he'd said Alex would be okay, he wasn't convinced.

And neither was she.

Later that afternoon Alex paced the mill parking lot, waiting for the chief who'd sent him a text that he wanted to meet. He probably didn't want to humiliate Alex by asking for his gun and badge at the station in front of Agent Trotter, Quinn and Nicole.

No, Alex was overthinking this. He hadn't been released from his duties. He was just placed on temporary leave. Alex would have done the same thing if he'd been chief and one of his guys put a witness in jeopardy.

We work better as a team. Her words haunted him. She was right: they did make a good team. In the three days since they'd known each other he felt closer to Nicole than he did to anyone else. He'd become an expert at keeping people at a distance since Jessica's death. Yet somehow Nicole had breached his defenses.

Then Agent Trotter's accusation taunted him: *lady, you've got a bad case of transference.*

Is that what this was for Nicole? She clung to Alex like an anchor—was it because her life had been threatened over and over again? No, he knew in his heart it was more than that. He hoped it was more than that.

He fingered the silver cross around his neck. *God, please help me do the right thing here.*

Was he helping her by giving into his feelings? Or would it be more honorable to keep his distance until the case was resolved, and then ask her out on a date?

"What are you talking about?" he muttered. A date, seriously? After everything they'd been through?

Theirs was a dysfunctional relationship, one that had little chance of developing once the danger that brought them together was no longer in the picture.

The chief pulled up the long driveway and for half a second Alex considered he'd made himself an easy target if the chief was, in fact, in collusion with the killer. Alex couldn't ignore that possibility, especially after the chief's strategic move to take Alex off the case.

Chief Roth got out of his car. "How's your head, son?"

"I'm fine."

"Are you? Because the Donovan I know wouldn't have taken a witness with a bounty on her head to a dangerous meeting without backup."

"Here." Alex pulled his gun off his belt and reached for his badge.

"Hang on." The chief stepped back and put out his hand. "You're not quitting on me."

"I'm on leave. I figured you'd want these."

"Don't be ridiculous. I put you on leave, both to get Trotter off my back, and so you could focus on other things that are important to you—like protecting Nicole Harris."

"But you need me to help solve the case."

"I need you to keep the witness safe, and it's impossible to do that while chasing leads and conducting interviews."

Alex clipped his gun back to his belt. "Speaking of which…"

"Nicole and your brother gave their statements. He's a sharp kid. Got the make and model of the vehicle before it took off. No surprise it matches the truck that bumped you last night."

"And Nicole?"

"Didn't remember much. Apparently she had the wind knocked out of her when you tackled her?"

"Gut instinct."

"And a good one. That's why I need you to stick with her. I'll forward information to you about the case and we can brainstorm, but you need to do that from the safety of wherever you're staying. I dug up background on Artie Wagner. He had a sheet. I've emailed it to you."

"Thanks."

"Okay, now I've got a question for you and I need a straight answer. Why didn't you call me to back you up?"

Alex sighed and glanced across the property, toward the harbor. "I thought I could handle it on my own."

"Tell me another story."

Alex eyed the chief.

"Try the truth this time," the chief said.

Now that Alex stood face-to-face with Chief Roth, the one man who'd encouraged Alex, had faith in him when Alex first moved back to Waverly Harbor, Alex couldn't say the words.

He couldn't call him a traitor to his face.

"Ah," Chief Roth said. "You thought I was playing for the other side."

Alex glanced at the ground, unable to confirm the accusation.

"Because the driver came after you when you left my house," the chief stated. "Okay, good."

"Good?" Alex eyed him.

"Sure, that means your detective skills haven't been completely derailed by your feelings for Nicole Harris."

"Wait, you're not angry with me?"

"For what? You considered the information in front of you and formed a logical conclusion. I would have formed the same one, although I won't tell Gayle about your suspicions. Wouldn't want to hurt her feelings."

"I'm sorry. It's where I go when I'm working a case."

"That's why you're a great detective."

"I can't figure out how the driver found us last night and how the killer found Artie today. Quinn didn't follow me, he tracked my phone. That number isn't public, so that's not how the killer tracked me." Alex whipped his head around and eyed his car.

"Let's search it," the chief said, picking up on the direction of Alex's thoughts.

They started to search the interior of the car. "Wait, I always lock it. Let's check the outside." Alex dropped to the ground and felt beneath the undercarriage on the driver's side.

"I'm afraid if I get down there I'll never get up," Chief Roth said.

"I got this."

Alex went to the other side of the car and dropped down. He ran his hands along the cool metal and felt a small transmitting device. He snapped it off. "Got it!"

Chief Roth didn't answer.

"Chief?" Alex glanced beneath the car to his right.

And saw the chief lying on the ground.

ELEVEN

Alex rushed around the front of the truck to the chief, who gripped his shoulder.

"What happened?" the chief asked.

The soft pfft of a silenced gunshot hit the ground beside Alex.

"Come on." Alex helped the chief to the other side of the truck.

"Knew I shoulda worn my vest this morning," the chief joked. "I think I need to retire. You want a promotion?"

Alex examined the chief's gunshot wound. "Let's get you to a hospital."

The chief gripped Alex's jacket sleeve. "Wait. The Feds will see this as one more example of our incompetence. Go get Nicole and take her someplace safe."

"I'm not leaving you here."

"That's an order, detective."

"I'm on leave, remember?" Alex whipped open the car door and helped him onto the backseat. Staying low, Alex climbed across the passenger seat and got behind the wheel. He started the car and shifted to Reverse, hoping to get far enough away from the shooter so Alex could pop his head up to see where he was going.

"Hold on!" Alex spun the wheel and they did a 180. He shoved the car in Drive and hit the gas, speeding out of the mill parking lot and up the hill toward town. The shooter wouldn't follow him into a public place, at least Alex hoped he wouldn't.

"Take me to the medical center," the chief said.

"I need to get you to Skagit Valley Hospital."

"My injury isn't life threatening. Drop me at the center and get back to the witness before the shooter finds her."

Alex rolled down his window, slapped the emergency light on the roof of his truck and headed for the medical center. He didn't care if he drew attention. Alex had to get Chief

Roth to a doctor before he lost too much blood.

"Slow down, Alex. Don't want you getting in a fender bender."

"We're a minute away, tops."

"Get Nicole to a safe place and call me tomorrow. And Alex?"

"Yes, sir?"

"This was not your fault."

As Nicole sat in the backseat of Quinn's fancy SUV with tinted windows she eyed Alex, who stared out his side window deep in thought.

"I thought the chief was going to be okay," she said.

"He will be."

"The expression on your face tells a different story."

Alex glared at the back of his brother's head. "I could have found your secret hideaway on my own."

"Uh, probably not," Quinn said from the front seat. "Besides, since you're both in the back, no one can see you."

"Are you headed to work after you drop us off?"

"You're that anxious to get rid of me? Afraid Nicole might realize I'm the better catch?"

"No, little brother, I don't want to see you shot and killed in front of me."

The car fell silent. Nicole pieced it together: Alex blamed himself for the chief being shot and would blame himself if anything happened to his brother. He probably still felt guilty about abandoning Quinn as a teenager, leaving him to be emotionally abused by their stepmother.

"How much longer?" Alex said.

"Not long."

"That's specific."

"Alex," she said, hoping to derail the argument she felt coming. "What's happening with the case?"

He looked at her with such defeat in his eyes. "Who's got time to work the case? I'm just trying to keep everybody I care about alive."

He gazed back out the side window. She understood his frustration but refused to let him drown in self-recrimination. Carefully sliding her hand across the leather seat, she laid it gently over his. Although he wouldn't look at her, he entwined his fingers with hers.

"I've ordered dinner for us," Quinn said.

"Ordered from where?" Alex questioned.

"Don't worry. My neighbor doubles as my personal chef. She's making us a four-course meal. Hope you like salmon."

"Quinn, I don't want more innocent people to get hurt."

"Billy can handle herself, trust me."

"Billy is a woman's name?" Nicole asked.

"Nickname. Great cook. She lives in the coach house next door."

"What does she do when she's not cooking for you?" Nic asked, trying to keep the conversation light.

"She's a freelancer. Does some event planning for groups that book space at my properties. She's a multitalented woman."

"Oh, really?" Alex said.

"Get your mind out of the gutter. It's not like that."

"How'd you meet her?" Alex asked.

"On a search-and-rescue call."

"Search and rescue?" Alex questioned.

"Yes, dear brother. My life isn't limited to running a business and charming women."

Alex eyed Quinn like he didn't recognize him. "When did you start doing search and rescue?"

"Stop grilling me like a suspect."

Quinn pulled up to a tall, iron gate and entered a code on the keypad. The gates opened and Nicole rolled down her window to get a better look. Although it was dark outside she could make out the gorgeous grounds covered in colorful rhododendrons and juniper.

They pulled up to a modest, two-story house with a dormered roof and wooden front porch. She expected it to be bigger, more ostentatious. She got out of the car and studied the home, so unlike its owner. Alex came around and offered his hand. She took it and he led her up the stairs onto the porch. Quinn pressed another code by the front door and they went inside.

She paused in the entryway trying to cover her shock. For some reason she thought

Quinn's house would be elegant and refined. Instead, rustic wood furniture accented a large great room with hardwood floors, throw rugs and a beautiful rock fireplace.

A tall, slender woman with dark hair and a wide smile stepped around the corner to greet them. "Hi, Quinn."

They shared a quick hug and he turned to Alex and Nicole.

"Alex, Nicole, this is my friend Billy."

They shook hands.

"Thanks for being available on such short notice," Quinn said to Billy.

"Are you kidding? I wouldn't miss a chance to meet the hero big brother." She winked at Alex and motioned everyone into the great room. "Help yourselves to raspberry iced tea and fruit while I finish dinner."

"I'll help," Quinn said, following Billy into the kitchen through a swinging door.

Nicole sensed lightness about Quinn she hadn't noticed before. She wondered if Billy held a special place in his heart.

Alex wandered through the great room. As

he picked up photographs and knickknacks, a look of fascination spread across his face.

"You look like you've never been here before," Nicole said.

"I haven't." He glanced at her with a frown. "I had no idea." He held up a cheesy gold trophy. "This was mine, from tenth grade track and field day. I figured Sophia had tossed it when she moved out."

"When did she move out?"

Alex sighed and continued to analyze knickknacks. "About five years ago. Quinn and I didn't know it at the time. After Jess died, and I came back to lick my wounds, I found out Sophia had emptied Dad's bank account, filed for divorce and trashed the house, looking for valuables, I guess. He didn't put up much resistance. He'd been living alone for six months when I showed up. Then we found out why she left." Alex turned to Nicole. "Dad had cancer and she didn't want to take care of him."

"He had cancer and didn't tell you?"

"Nope. I guess he didn't want to worry me, us. Quinn didn't know, either."

"But it's a small town and people talk."

"Sophia was a master at keeping secrets. Dad didn't want to admit he'd failed at being a good husband so he told people in town she was away visiting family. After a while I think folks suspected, but respected his privacy."

"He thought he'd failed at being a good husband? I doubt that very much."

"Why do you say that?" He suddenly looked at her. "You didn't even know him."

"I know you. Only a very special man could have raised such wonderful sons."

"Wonderful?" Quinn said, entering the great room. "Did she just call me wonderful?"

"Oh, boy, you shouldn't have said that," Billy offered, following close behind. "He's already got an ego the size of an elephant."

"An elephant?" Quinn said. "Gee, thanks."

Billy wandered to the coffee table where a pitcher and four glasses were set up. "Hey, we all know your ego is your bulletproof vest. Who wants raspberry tea?"

"I'll have some," Nicole said, fascinated by Billy's analysis of Quinn's ego.

Alex's phone vibrated. "It's the chief." He wandered into the hallway.

Billy handed Nicole a glass of tea and offered a sympathetic smile. "I heard you've had a traumatic experience."

"Yeah, more than one in the last few days."

"I've gotta check on something," Quinn said, and went back into the kitchen.

"Was it something I said?" Nicole joked.

"He sensed an emotional moment and needed to escape," Billy explained.

"You two, are you…?"

"Nah, it's not like that. We're good friends."

"Oh, because I got the impression—"

"That he's a ladies' man? He likes to flirt, that's for sure."

"I was going to say that he's different around you."

Billy poured herself an iced tea. "It's this house. It's his refuge. No one ever comes here."

"No one but you."

"I'm his cook and general caretaker. I keep an eye on things." Billy glanced at Nicole. "I owe Quinn. He saved my life."

"How— I'm sorry, I shouldn't pry."

"It's okay. Hiking accident. My husband and I were stranded in the mountains for two days in the North Cascades. Quinn was part of the search-and-rescue team. His was the first face I saw when they came to get us."

"Where's your husband now?"

"He didn't make it."

"I'm so sorry."

"Thanks. It happened a while ago."

But Nicole read the grief on Billy's face. She flopped down on the sofa and Nicole sat in a nearby rocking chair.

"I took care of Rick for eighteen hours, tried to keep him hydrated and calm. But he had a head injury and, well, we were out there too long without medical attention." She glanced at the door leading to the kitchen. "I think Quinn blames himself for not getting there sooner."

"The Donovans and their guilt," Nicole muttered.

"That woman did a major number on her stepsons."

"So, you know about her?"

"A little. When I woke up at the hospital,

Quinn was there. We became friends. I was in shock after Rick died. His family blamed me. I'm an only child and my parents are gone so…I was essentially alone."

"And Quinn saved you again, didn't he?"

"Yep. Those boys are really good at saving the damsel in distress."

"True," Nicole said. "But who's going to save them?"

She and Billy shared a knowing look.

"I wish I could," Billy said. "But anytime I get close to crossing the line, Quinn brings home a new girlfriend for dinner."

"Tell me he doesn't make you cook," Nicole said, aghast.

"He does, but I understand why he does it."

"Then explain it to me."

"He's keeping me at a distance. I think emotional intimacy is more terrifying than death for Quinn. I don't take it personally."

"You're a strong woman," Nicole said.

"It took a long time to get here." Billy held out her glass in a toast. "To strong women."

They clinked glasses just as Quinn walked in.

"What did I miss?" he said, going to the coffee table and pouring an iced tea.

"Girl talk," Nicole said.

"That can't be good."

Alex wandered into the great room wearing a pensive expression.

"What's wrong?" Quinn asked.

"Edward Lange's sister is going to the press, accusing the department of negligence in her brother's murder investigation. Quinn, do you have a television?"

"Sure." He grabbed a remote control and pressed a button.

The wall parted to reveal a flat-screen TV. Quinn turned on the local news. As they went through the top stories of the day, Nicole gripped her iced tea glass and studied Alex's distant expression.

"In other news, Abigail Woods, computer magnate Edward Lange's sister, is accusing Waverly Harbor police of mishandling her brother's murder investigation."

Abigail Woods's image flashed on the screen as the reporter interviewed her. "I don't understand why the local police won't turn over the investigation to the FBI. It's obvious they have the resources and experience to find my brother's killer, but the local police department won't give up jurisdiction."

"What reason have they given you, Mrs. Woods?"

"None, which makes me wonder if it's simple negligence or some kind of conspiracy."

"Are you inferring the local police were involved in your brother's death?"

"I don't know what to think anymore." Abigail lowered her eyes. Her husband, David, handed her a handkerchief from behind.

The camera refocused on the reporter who Nicole realized stood outside the Waverly Harbor police station. The reporter looked directly into the camera. "If you have any information regarding Edward Lange's murder please contact the FBI." They flashed a phone number on the screen. "The Woodses are offering a ten thousand dollar reward for information leading to the killer's identity. This is Amy Rogers with Channel 5 News."

The program went back to the anchors in the newsroom. Nicole studied Alex, who hadn't moved or taken a breath during the news report.

Quinn clicked off the television. Billy and Nicole shared a worried look, then glanced at Quinn who hadn't taken his eyes off his brother.

"Alex?" Quinn prompted.

Alex snapped his attention to the group. "It's going to create chaos. False leads will pour in because people want the cash reward. I've got to solve this thing before anyone else gets hurt."

Alex stormed into the front hallway and grabbed his backpack. "Quinn, do you have a computer I can use? I need something more powerful than my tablet," he said from the doorway.

"Sure, but dinner's almost ready."

"I can't eat right now."

Nicole went to Alex and gently touched his arm. "You'll think better with food in your stomach."

He looked at her with defeat in his eyes.

"Half an hour isn't going to prevent you from solving this case." She interlaced her fingers with his and led him toward the dining area, surprised that he didn't fight her.

After an awkwardly quiet dinner, Nicole convinced Alex to accept help from her and Quinn, while Billy finished up the dishes. Nicole had been at the scene of the murder and possibly remembered something in her subconscious that could help identify the killer, and Quinn was trying to offer support in any way he could. He obviously loved his brother very much and couldn't stand seeing him in such pain.

The advanced computer setup in Quinn's office surprised Nicole. Besides being a successful businessman Quinn apparently was a tech geek, as well.

As they dug deeper into the backgrounds of potential suspects, Nicole realized Alex's short-tempered responses were hurting his relationship with his brother.

"Why don't you see if Billy needs help?" she suggested to Quinn.

With a nod he ambled across the room and hesitated at the door. "If you need anything I'll be in the kitchen."

The comment was directed at Alex, but he didn't respond.

"Thanks," Nicole offered.

Once they were alone, she put a comforting hand on Alex's back. His shoulders sagged as he leaned forward in his chair. "I can't do this, not from here."

"What do you need, then?"

"I need to see the evidence they processed at the scene, but that can't happen. It's not safe to leave."

"What do you think the evidence will show?"

"Not sure. I've got two viable suspects from Lange's work. Gerry Walker and Adam Fluke. The detective in Seattle hasn't been able to track them down."

"And you think it's one of them because...?"

"They were both on the Tech Link team. I think this all has to do with the launch of that software."

"The reporter did make it sound like Tech Link was problematic. But Edward didn't seem like the type of man to hide his failures. He actually embraced them as learning experiences."

"An admirable quality."

Yes, and one she wished Alex could embrace.

"You're thinking either or both of those men could be in Waverly Harbor?"

He nodded. "If I could link them to the murder that could solve this thing and get the rest of the world off our backs."

"Where is the evidence?" she asked.

"A state lab about an hour from here." He stood, took her hand and gave it a squeeze. "You'll be safe here with Quinn."

"It's nearly eight. Aren't they closed?"

"I'm hoping my ID will get me access."

"And if it doesn't?"

"Quinn!" Alex called, ignoring her question.

"You're going to break in?" she pushed.

Quinn and Billy came into the office.

"I've got to check something out," Alex said. "Can you keep Nicole safe for a few hours?"

"No," Nicole protested. "I'm not letting you go by yourself."

Alex stared at his brother, waiting for an answer.

"Where are you going?" Quinn asked.

"He's going to break into the crime lab to look through evidence," Nicole said.

"Well, let's go." Quinn downed his iced tea and placed it on a nearby table.

"Hang on, this is a solo job," Alex said.

"You'll need a getaway driver, plus a lookout," Quinn argued. "I'm going."

"So am I," Nicole said.

"I'll drive," Billy said, grabbing a shoulder bag by the front closet. "They won't recognize my Jetta."

"No one's coming with me and that's an order," Alex protested.

"Think about this, Alex," Nicole said. "The Feds are looking for us, the press is everywhere, and they probably have the description of Quinn's cars, right?"

Alex eyed her, but didn't answer.

"My back windows are tinted," Billy said. She pointed to Alex and Nicole. "You can sit in back and Quinn in front."

"I'll wear a hat and sunglasses," Quinn offered.

"Oh, that's not obvious," Alex shot back.

"Hey—" Nicole grabbed his arm "—you can't do this alone and that's okay. Let us help."

"I won't involve innocent civilians."

Quinn walked up to his brother, closer than she'd ever seen them before. She thought he was going to say something profound to Alex. Instead, he smiled. "I haven't been innocent since the fifth grade when I borrowed one of Sophia's necklaces and gave it to Susie Turner so she'd go steady with me."

Alex raised an eyebrow. "Borrowed?"

"Let's go, big brother."

Emotionally exhausted, Nicole dozed en route. They arrived at the forensics office and Alex tried to get Nicole to stay in the car but she refused. She could help him identify critical evidence that could reveal the killer's identity. He finally acquiesced.

Quinn brought a laptop in case they needed information about the building. He and Billy waited in the car, parked behind a cluster of trees bordering the property. They would text Alex if they saw anyone approach the building.

Luckily his key card worked and they got inside. Alex used a flashlight to locate a box marked *Edward Lange Homicide*. Alex and Nicole put on latex gloves and pulled plastic bags out of the box, analyzing each one. Nicole pretended the blood smearing some of the items didn't bother her. She had to stay strong and not let Alex think this would further traumatize her.

"What's this?" Nicole asked, holding up a bag with a man's gold, chain link bracelet.

"I assumed it was Edward's bracelet, ripped off during the struggle."

"He didn't wear jewelry. Ever."

"Are you sure?"

She looked at Alex. "Ruby said it distracted him. He was adamant about it."

Alex studied the bracelet.

"Are you going to take it?" she asked.

"No, when this goes to trial I don't want accusations of mishandling of evidence causing a mistrial. Everything needs to go back in the box when we're done." He picked up another bag containing Edward's bloody cell phone. "Wish I could access everything in here."

"You can."

He looked at her. "I can't take it out of the bag."

"I can access it using Achilles Guard."

"Come again?"

"It's a file sharing program Edward created. His phone activity, internet, everything is synced in Achilles Guard."

Suddenly the lights clicked on. Alex pressed his forefinger to his lips and led Nicole behind a tower of boxes.

Her heart pounded against her chest. Why didn't Quinn alert them someone was coming? And what was a forensics tech doing here at this time of night?

With a hand cradling the back of her head, Alex guided her cheek against his chest. She crunched his shirt between her fingers struggling to calm the adrenaline rushing through her body. If they were caught, would Nicole and Alex be charged with breaking and entering? No, they didn't break in—he used his access card to get into the building. Yet he was temporarily suspended.

"This stuff shouldn't be out," a male voice said.

They'd found the Lange evidence she and Alex had been looking through.

"Somebody's been here," a second voice said.

"Or still is."

Silence rang in her ears. The men were searching for Alex and Nicole. A part of her wanted to jump out of her hiding spot to distract the men and protect Alex. What could a couple of forensic techs do to her besides call the police and charge her with breaking and entering? Alex, on the other hand, had been suspended and his department was accused of negligence. He could lose his job, his life in Waverly Harbor.

"Come on out!" a man called.

Nicole glanced at the window on her right and spotted the reflection of a man stalking down the aisle.

Pointing a gun.

Alex must have seen it, too, because he shifted Nicole protectively behind him. She placed her hands against his back and took a calming breath. His muscles tensed as he prepared to defend them.

Please, God, help us.

TWELVE

A car alarm blared through the window.

"We've gotta get out of here," one of the men ordered. "Grab it and let's go."

"Lock them in."

"Come on!"

A door slammed and Alex poked his head around the boxes. He turned to Nicole. "You okay?"

"Sure, sure."

But her eyes told a different story. She must have seen the man aiming a gun as he made his way through the lab. Taking her hand, Alex led her to the door and swiped his card.

The door wouldn't open. He scanned the room and pulled out his phone. "Quinn, we've got a problem."

"I didn't see them until the lights went on so I set off our car alarm."

"We're fine, but my key card doesn't work."

"Give me a second. I'll find schematics for the building to get you another way out."

Alex retried his key card. Nothing.

An earsplitting alarm bounced off the ceiling and walls. Nicole gripped his arm.

"Any time, little brother," Alex shouted into the phone.

"Men's restroom."

"I can't get out of the lab."

"You don't have to. There's a door in the southwest corner leading to a small hallway. Men's and women's bathrooms are down there. The men's has a window."

"Big enough for a person?"

"Big enough for Nicole."

Which meant Alex was going to be left behind. He couldn't worry about that. He had to get Nicole to safety.

"This way," he shouted, guiding her to the door leading to the small hallway. Once inside the bathroom he spotted the window, not too high, about the right size for Nicole to squeeze through. He unlocked it and flipped open the window.

He interlaced his fingers and she stepped into them. He hoisted her up and into the window. Once out, she called back to him. "Okay, come on! Wait, how are you going to fit?"

"Go!" He shut the window and called his brother on his cell. "Quinn, get her out of here."

"Will do. Call me when you're out and we'll pick you up."

"I'll probably be locked up, but thanks, anyway."

"Alex—"

"Text me when the state troopers show up."

Alex went back to the evidence box to analyze anything he'd missed. The clue was here, he knew it in his gut. As he rifled through the plastic bags his cell vibrated with a text. Quinn was letting him know the troopers were on the way.

"That was fast." He packed up the evidence and noticed the gold bracelet was missing.

He did another quick shuffle of evidence bags.

No bracelet. Which meant it must have belonged to the killer who came to the lab to recover it.

The alarm suddenly clicked off and silence rang in his ears. Alex slid the evidence box back in place and hid behind the tower of boxes in the corner.

The door clicked open. Alex sensed the state trooper enter the lab.

"Miller, 10-23, over," the trooper said.

An altercation with the trooper wasn't what Alex wanted but he didn't see that he had much choice. Yet he didn't want the cop to see his face or else they could accuse Alex of tampering with evidence.

Alex held his breath and waited. Sensing the deputy closing in, Alex shifted to the backside of the boxes and peered around to see the deputy walking in the other direction.

Alex lunged at the trooper's back, wrapping his arm around his neck. The gun flew out of the trooper's hand and he dug his fingers into Alex's arm to release the pressure on his windpipe. The hold was an effective move that rendered the victim unconscious without serious side affects.

If only the guy would surrender.

Instead, he kicked and thrashed, shoving Alex up against the wall. Alex applied more pressure and the trooper fell unconscious. Alex lowered him to the floor.

The sound of car doors slamming outside indicated backup had arrived. Instead of making a run for it, Alex pulled out his badge and kneeled beside Deputy Miller.

Two more deputies rushed into the lab. "Hands up!"

Alex flashed his badge over his shoulder. "Waverly Harbor P.D. We got a tip someone was going to break into the lab. When I got here the door was open and the deputy was on the ground."

He hoped the guy remained unconscious long enough for Alex to talk his way out of here.

The deputies holstered their firearms and one went to check Miller's pulse.

"He's okay," Alex said. He stood and

pulled out his cell. "I can't get bars in here. I need to call in." He headed for the door.

The second deputy blocked him.

Alex maintained a passive expression, although his insides were whirling like a tornado ripping through an Oklahoma cornfield.

"You think this has something to do with the Edward Lange homicide?" the trooper asked.

"That would be my guess. Can you check to make sure they didn't take off with the evidence box? I didn't have time." Alex nodded over his shoulder. "Was worried about the deputy."

"Yeah, thanks."

With a curt nod, Alex walked out of the building, glanced once over his shoulder...

And took off, hoping they didn't come looking for him. In seconds he reached the car and jumped into the backseat. Nicole wasn't there, neither was his brother.

"Where are they?" he asked Billy.

"He went to get Nicole."

Alex jerked open the door in time to see

Quinn pulling Nicole toward the car. Alex motioned for them to hurry. "Get in, quick."

She yanked away from Quinn, fisted her hands and glared at Alex. "Don't you ever—"

Alex pulled her close and kissed her, partly to keep her quiet, but mostly because he wanted to. He needed to.

"I thought we were in a hurry," Quinn said.

Alex released Nicole, who gazed up at him in shock.

"You can read me the riot act later. We've got to get out of here, okay?" he said.

With a nod, she climbed into the backseat and he slid in beside her. He closed the door and reached for her hand. Interlacing his fingers with hers, he said, "Let's go."

Nicole woke up with a start and looked around to get her bearings. She'd fallen asleep on the couch in Quinn's great room. Quinn was sleeping in a recliner in the corner and she assumed Billy had gone back to her house. Nicole wrapped a plaid throw around her shoulders and went to find Alex.

When she noticed light streaming through the bottom of the kitchen door she pushed it open and found Billy sound asleep, her head resting on folded arms on the kitchen counter. Nicole quietly backed out and continued her search. As she padded through the first floor, the glow of a computer screen illuminated the office off the main hallway.

She stepped up to the doorway and watched Alex for a few seconds before announcing her presence. If he'd been arrested last night or hurt in any way... Her stomach tangled in knots at the thought.

What she was feeling was not transference. It was deeper, more intense, and he felt it too or he wouldn't have kissed her.

"Hey," she said softly.

He swiveled in the office chair, leveling her with bloodshot, blue eyes.

"You don't look so good." She wandered closer and ran her fingers through his hair.

He closed his eyes and tipped his head back, reveling in her touch. "Mmm," he moaned.

"What time is it?"

"Three something." He opened his eyes. "Why are you up? Does my brother snore?"

"No, I just… I guess I knew you were up."

"Well, go back to sleep. I'm fine," he said.

"I want to help."

"You need to sleep." Holding her hand, he walked her back into the great room.

"I don't think I can," she whispered as they crossed the threshold, not wanting to wake Quinn. "Would you sit with me for a while?"

"Sure." Alex flopped down on the sofa and pulled Nicole beside him.

She curled her legs beneath her and leaned against his chest, listening to his strong, steady heartbeat. She hoped he didn't figure out her ulterior motive: to make him get a few hours of sleep so he didn't look so beaten.

"I love this," she whispered.

He held her tighter.

"I wish you could hold me like this forever," she added.

She traced her fingers across his chest, dreaming about a life with Alex. For once, there was potential for something greater than a lonely existence eating frozen dinners in front of the television.

She nuzzled his chest and drifted, imagining long walks along the harbor, laughter with friends and dinners at the chief's house.

There was no doubt in her mind. She had fallen in love.

Nicole's plan had worked. She'd awakened four hours later in Alex's arms on the sofa. She'd never felt more comfortable or more safe. But they didn't stay like that for long.

They got up, ate breakfast and spent the better part of the day going through Edward's personal files, sifting for clues. Alex had borrowed dress slacks and a button-down shirt from Quinn, so different from Alex's usual jeans, cotton shirt and leather jacket ensemble.

Luckily, Billy was about Nicole's size so she loaned Nicole jeans and a blouse. Quinn had gone to deal with a work crisis and Billy went back to her place.

"What do you think these initials stand for?" Alex asked her as they analyzed Edward's calendar.

"Saturday is TR, that stands for training. But who did he have on Friday?" She flipped the calendar backward and stared at the initials SR.

"I spoke with the Seattle detective. He finally caught up with the two suspects from Lange Enterprises, but they both have alibis."

"SR, SR," she whispered. "He had his own language sometimes. It's not initials, it's..." She looked at him. "Alex, it stands for 'sister.'"

"Are you sure?"

"Yeah, check this out." She pushed him aside and scrolled backward through Edward's calendar. "SR is on July 10, which was the company's 10 year anniversary. I helped Ruby plan this big celebration, but Edward was late because of a meeting with his sister."

"Abigail Woods," he said pensively.

"But I heard a man arguing with Edward at the lake house."

"Abigail could have hired someone."

"I guess, but the argument sounded personal and why would she kill her own brother? They seemed to have a pretty good relationship."

"Well." He leaned back in his chair and sighed. "There's the obvious reason."

"Money?"

He nodded. "Do you think she'd want to run Lange Industries? Or possibly sell it?"

"I don't know her that well, sorry."

"Let's do a little research." He typed Abigail's name into a search engine and her photo popped up along with news stories about Edward.

"And she pointed the finger at me," Nicole grumbled.

"It's a good distraction, as is putting up the reward. It makes her seem like a loving sister."

She slid a chair next to him and they spent another hour going through articles about Abigail Woods, encompassing everything from biographies about her upbringing, to notices about her volunteer work for Seattle Children's Hospital. They scanned her business profile and social networking pages, trying to find something, anything that could give them a clue as to motive. There were plenty of photos of Edward with his sister supporting her altruistic projects.

"They seemed to genuinely care about each other," Nicole said.

"Unlike me and my brother," Alex muttered.

"Hey, you two care about each other. You're just very different people. You have to know that Quinn would do anything for his big brother."

"We must not be talking about the same guy." He pulled out his phone.

"Who are you calling?"

"The chief. He needs to know about Abigail."

He held the phone to his ear. "Huh, it went right to voice mail."

"Do you think his injury was more serious than it looked?"

"I'll try the house." He made the call and glanced up at Nicole with worry in his eyes. "Hello, Gayle, it's Alex. I need to… What? When? That makes no sense. They have no cause for… I'm sure he'll be fine. He hasn't done anything wrong…. Okay. Have him call me when he gets home. Thanks."

Alex slowly lowered the phone.

"What happened?" Nicole said.

He glanced up with a confused expression. "The Feds brought the chief in for questioning."

"What? Why?"

"It's got to be a power play. The Feds want this case, they want you, and if they accuse the chief of impropriety and Waverly P.D. is off the case, it leaves no one in charge, giving the FBI the opportunity to take over."

"But he didn't do anything wrong. He was shot!"

The front door slammed, sending a vibration through the wall between the hallway and the office.

Quinn rushed into the office doorway with a panicked look on his face.

Alex stood. "What is it?"

"They put out a bulletin on you claiming you kidnapped Nicole."

"That's ridiculous," she said.

"It's good strategy to find us." Alex motioned with his hand. "Quinn, give me your car keys and we'll get out of here."

"And go where?" Quinn said.

"Doesn't matter."

"Forget it, no."

"I don't want you involved in this."

"I'm already involved." Quinn walked away.

"Quinn!" Alex said sternly. He started after him and hesitated in the doorway, glancing over his shoulder at Nicole.

"Go," she said. "I'll keep surfing the Net for stuff on Abigail Woods."

He disappeared into the hallway in search of his brother, and Nicole settled in the chair. Too much was happening, and it was happening too fast. The chief had been detained, and the cops were after Alex for kidnapping Nicole? She couldn't stand that her predicament was putting good people in jeopardy like Alex and Quinn.

But knowledge was power, and if she could find solid evidence implicating Abigail Woods, that could put an end to the threat on Nicole's life. Which made her wonder... why was Abigail's henchman still after Nicole? Did they want her dead because they thought she knew something that could implicate Abigail?

With renewed energy she scanned through Edward's smartphone, hoping to find something that would explain Abigail's motivation for killing her brother.

She scanned through photos of Edward with his business manager and Edward with his brainstorming team on the Tech-Link project. She zoomed in on their faces. They all looked happy, which meant the photo must have been taken at the launch party. She scrolled through photo after photo, and landed on a photo of David Woods with his arm around Edward. Abigail stood in the background with a scowl on her face.

"She doesn't look happy," Nic whispered.

Suddenly the intercom buzzed, startling Nicole. She went into the hallway as Alex and Quinn approached the intercom. Quinn pressed a button and Agent Trotter's face popped up on the screen.

"FBI." He flashed his badge into the camera. "We have a warrant to search the premises."

THIRTEEN

"They're looking for me," Nicole said, guilt ripping through her.

"For us," Alex corrected. "So they can lock me up and interrogate you."

"Won't they try to find Lange's killer?" Quinn asked.

"Their priority is their investigation of Edward Lange. If they discover the killer in the process that's an added bonus." He took her hands in his. "You're not safe until we find the killer."

The intercom buzzed again, making Nicole's shoulders jerk.

Alex glanced at Quinn. "I can't protect her if I'm locked up. What's out back? Could we take a boat out of here?"

"No, they'll hear you. I have another idea." He motioned them into his office and moved a large Queen Anne chair away from the wall.

"This is no time to redecorate, Quinn."

"You're hilarious."

Quinn kneeled down, peeled the rug off the floor and popped out a large floorboard. He looked over his shoulder at Alex and Nicole. "Should be room enough for two. It'll be a tight squeeze but somehow I don't think you'll mind," he said with a wry smile.

"What's it for?" Alex said, with suspicion in his voice.

"Nothing illegal. Come on, stop arguing and get down there."

Alex climbed down the small ladder, then Nicole followed. Alex's hands gripped her waist to steady her as she descended into the storage chamber.

The intercom buzzed again.

"There's a camping light to your right," Quinn pointed.

Alex hesitated.

"They won't be able to see the light once I put the carpeting over the floorboards," Quinn said.

Quinn slid the hardwood board back in

place. Light peered through the cracks in the wood. Quinn replaced the throw rug, bathing them in darkness. They heard Quinn call for Billy, who was in the kitchen.

Alex clicked on the light and they studied the boxes, each marked with their contents. One was marked *Alex's Accomplishments*.

"I had no idea," he whispered.

The thump of the chair above them made Nicole duck.

"It's okay." Alex held her against his chest and stroked her hair.

Nicole realized she was hiding much like she hid her brother and sister when they were little. Back then Nic had been terrified, cowering in her own closet, waiting for the monster to pull out the belt and teach her a lesson.

Yet right now in Alex's arms she wasn't terrified, she was determined—determined to protect herself and Alex.

The sound of footsteps echoed above them. The agents had entered the office.

"If they weren't here, why do you have pictures of the Woodses on your computer?" Agent Trotter asked.

Nicole hugged Alex tighter, berating herself for not hitting the escape key.

"I'm researching business investors," Quinn said. "I figured Abigail Woods is going to come into a lot of money."

"Man, you are cold," Agent Trotter said.

"So I've been told more than once by my brother."

"Ya know what I think? I think he was here and he told you where he's going next."

"I wouldn't know. We're not exactly close."

"You followed him out to the church where Artie Walker was killed."

"Alex owes me money," Quinn joked. "It was time he paid up."

Nicole clung to Alex fearing his little brother's attitude was going to get him into trouble.

Scuffling echoed through the floorboards.

"I found her in the kitchen," another voice said.

"Let her go," Quinn demanded.

More scuffling was followed by a crash.

"Don't!" Billy cried.

A thud. Then nothing.

Footsteps pounded across the office.

A door slammed.

Silence.

Did they leave? If so, why hadn't Quinn removed the carpet and floorboard so Nicole and Alex could climb out?

Then she had the grim thought that the agents took Quinn and Billy and perhaps left other agents in the house just in case she and Alex showed up. Which meant she and Alex could be down here for a long time.

Seconds stretched like hours. Alex gently stroked her hair. She wasn't sure how he could remain so calm considering the chaos that had raged above them.

"Should we get out?" she whispered.

"Let's give it a few minutes. Just to be safe."

Light peeked through the floorboards. Someone had removed the carpet. Nicole took a slow, deep breath. She was done being afraid, and if a federal agent was the one to pop off the floorboard, then so be it.

Instead, Billy shifted the floorboard off the opening and motioned them out. Nicole went first.

"What happened?" Nicole asked.

Billy hugged herself. "They took Quinn."

"Why?" Alex said, climbing out and shoving the board back in place.

"He did it for me," Billy whispered.

"Shh," Nicole said, stroking her arm. "Tell us what happened."

"He picked a fight with the agent to distract him from me."

"Why would he need to distract them from you?" Alex asked.

Billy shook her head. "My husband was a criminal. Quinn probably worried that they'd use his crimes against me somehow so I'd tell them where you were." With teary eyes, Billy looked up at Alex. "They shot Quinn with a Taser because...because he was protecting me."

"Nicole, take Billy into the kitchen and make her a cup of tea. I'll be there in a few minutes."

Nicole remarked that Alex seemed way too calm given the circumstances. As Nicole led Billy away she noticed books and files strewn across the office, and a ceramic vase shattered on the floor in the hallway. She needed to stay calm for Billy's sake and convince the woman that everything was going to be okay.

Nicole settled Billy at the kitchen counter and heated water in a teakettle.

"I feel like some mistakes haunt you forever, you know?" Billy whispered.

"I know exactly what you mean." Nicole found the tea selection and grabbed some mugs. "You shouldn't blame yourself for what happened. Quinn wouldn't want that."

Billy shrugged. "Old habits die hard."

Kind of like Nicole blaming herself for her father's abusive ways.

A few minutes later Nicole steeped tea for her and Billy, hoping that Alex would join them. He didn't. Nicole struggled to stay positive and make conversation with Billy, but her mind was elsewhere, worrying about Alex's ability to help his brother.

"Go see how he's doing," Billy said suddenly.

"What?"

"I can tell you're worried about Alex. Go on."

"Thanks."

Gripping the mug, she padded through the

kitchen into the hallway and froze in the doorway to the office. Alex stood with his back to her, raking his hand through thick, wavy hair.

"You have no idea where they took him? Uh-huh. No, don't do that, you could get in trouble. I'll figure something out. Thanks."

He lowered the phone and stared out the window. He was so still, so quiet and she wanted to go to him.

Then she realized he was praying.

She clenched her mug even tighter and closed her eyes, saying a prayer herself. *Dear Lord, I know I'm probably not worthy to ask, but please help Alex. I love him. I'd do anything to help him. Amen.*

Alex cleared his throat and she opened her eyes. He shook his head and eyed his phone as if trying to figure out who to call.

"Alex?"

He turned and her breath caught at the sight of his lost expression.

"What is it?" she said.

"I spoke with our secretary and she has no idea where they've taken Quinn."

"I'm so sorry." She wanted to go to him, but instinct told her he needed space.

"I just...I've gotta do something." His gaze drifted to the phone in his hand. "He's my kid brother. I can't abandon him again."

"I'm sure he doesn't see it that way."

"How could he not?"

The guilt in his voice shot pain across her chest. It felt as if she was experiencing his feelings, his angst.

With ever fiber of her being she wanted to ease his pain.

"He kept my old trophies and ribbons," he said, his soft voice tinged with amazement. "And what did I do? I involved him in a murder investigation, and now he's in custody."

"Hey, you've kept me safe," she said, walking up to him and taking his hand.

He looked at her and cracked a sad, defeated smile. "Yeah, but for how long?"

His cell phone vibrated and he released her hand. "Donovan. Yeah? When?"

She wandered across the room and picked up her mug. Alex could have made his way out of the storage area, turned himself in and saved his brother from being taken by the Feds, but he didn't because he was committed to protecting Nicole.

He sacrificed his brother's safety for Nicole and the result of that action was tearing him apart. If Alex didn't have to watch over Nicole he could finish his investigation of Abigail Woods—he could find Edward's killer.

Frustration tangled her stomach in knots at the thought of Alex having to choose between playing bodyguard for Nicole and protecting his family. She wouldn't put him through that kind of pain any longer. Hadn't he lost enough—his father, his girlfriend and now Quinn, who was in trouble with the FBI?

It was suddenly clear what she had to do.

She loved Alex more intensely than she'd ever loved another human being in her life. With that in mind she wandered into the kitchen and strategized her next move.

Billy looked up. "What's going on?"

"I need your help."

Alex spent the next few hours calling anyone he could think of who might be able to help get Quinn released from FBI custody. He almost called Agent Banks, but thought better of it, assuming the decision to take Quinn must have come from the top.

Exhausted from the adrenaline rush of hiding beneath the floorboards, Nicole had gone to lie down in the guest room. That was two hours ago.

Which was probably a good thing. He didn't want to upset her further by witnessing his utter and complete frustration. She would easily sense the tension coursing through Alex's body. In the past few days they'd grown incredibly close, developing a connection that allowed her to know what Alex was thinking, how he was feeling.

Jessica was the only other person who'd been able to get that close and it had taken her two years.

No, his and Nicole's relationship wasn't a typical case of transference. It wasn't transference at all. They both knew it.

But there was no sense talking about how they felt given the current situation. Later, when the case was solved, Nicole was no longer in mortal danger and Quinn was back in his home....

Quinn. Alex realized that Nicole had somehow brought the brothers together, making Alex see another side of Quinn, the little brother who was a search-and-rescue volunteer, a computer genius. A brother who kept mementos under the floorboards where they'd be safe. Quinn had given Nicole and Alex refuge and followed Alex to the church for the meeting with Artie because Quinn was looking out for his big brother. He loved Alex even though Alex seemed to repeatedly let Quinn down.

"I have to get him released," he muttered.

He was about to surrender and call Agent Banks, when the front door opened.

"Hello?" Quinn called.

Alex jumped up from the desk in the office and raced into the hallway. Billy practically bowled Alex over as she bolted out of the kitchen and launched herself at Quinn. He gave her an awkward hug then let go.

"Could you get me some ice?" Quinn asked. "My head's killing me."

"Sure." Billy rushed into the kitchen.

"They let you go?" Alex said.

"You sound disappointed." Quinn wandered into the great room.

"Quinn."

His little brother turned around and looked at Alex. Heart pounding, Alex gave Quinn a quick hug, one which Quinn promptly broke.

Quinn backed up and collapsed on the sofa. "You missed me, huh?"

"I was out of my mind. I couldn't figure out how to help you and it was my fault because I involved you in the first place."

Billy rushed into the great room with an ice bag. "Here." She sat beside him and started to place the ice pack on his head, but he took it from her.

"Thanks." He held it in his hand and glanced at Alex. "For the record, I'm an adult, Alex. I made the choice to help you. None of this was your fault."

"What did they want?"

"Who knows? They locked me in an interrogation room but didn't ask any questions. It's like they were using me to get at something, probably get at you."

"But why suddenly let you go?"

"It was weird. About half an hour ago they said it was time to go, put me in a Suburban and drove me back. It's almost like they got whatever they were after."

"They're not after anything but information and Nicole, and she's asleep in the guest room."

"Um, actually…" Billy said.

Alex and Quinn looked at her.

"Billy?" Quinn said with warning in his voice.

"She said it was the only way to keep you guys safe."

"What are you talking about?" Alex asked, fearing her answer.

"She borrowed my car and went to meet with the FBI."

It was the right thing to do, Nicole told herself as she gripped the steering wheel of Billy's car and headed to the rendezvous with the FBI.

She wouldn't continue to hurt Alex by being in his life. The devastation on his face when they'd taken Quinn broke her heart. How much did this man have to suffer to keep Nicole safe? The FBI had a team of men who would protect her. This is what they'd wanted from the beginning: to have Nicole in their custody. So what if they weren't looking out for her best interest?

All she cared about was Alex's physical and emotional well-being.

Alex, the man she'd fallen in love with. Talk about bad timing.

Her cell phone rang and she eyed it on the seat beside her. It was Ruby. She pressed the speakerphone button.

"Hey, friend," Nicole said.

"How's it going?"

"I've been better. I'm headed to a meeting with the FBI."

"What? I thought you were working with the local police."

Nicole glanced in her rearview and spotted a sedan closing in on her. She glanced at the speedometer. She was already going five miles over the speed limit.

"Nic?"

"Sorry, yeah, I was working with local police, but the FBI needs to interview me."

"That sounds serious."

"They've been wanting to take me into custody since Edward's death but—"

The sedan clipped her back bumper and she yelped.

"What's going on?" Ruby asked.

"Some guy just hit the car. What is his problem?"

"Is he drunk?"

"I don't—"

The sedan hit her again. She lost control of the car, slammed on the brake and swerved…landing in a ditch.

"Nicole!" Ruby shouted.

Gripping the wheel, Nicole calmed her racing heart. "I'm fine."

Yet it was awfully coincidental that this guy would bump her off the road as she was on her way to meet with the FBI. "Ruby, if anything weird happens—"

"What do you mean, weird?"

"You have to find Alex—"

Her door swung open. A firm hand gripped her arm and yanked her out of the car.

FOURTEEN

Nicole was gone.

On some level it made sense, Alex thought, staring out the great room window at the lake. After seeing the Feds take Quinn, Nicole must have realized Alex wasn't able to protect her anymore than he could protect his little brother. Or Dad. Or Jessica.

Maybe she didn't feel the visceral connection between them, a connection he didn't think possible after he'd lost Jessica.

Apparently Nicole had weighed her options and chose survival over love. There, he finally admitted it to himself. He'd fallen in love with her only to lose her due to his own incompetence.

"Whoa, whoa, whoa, where are you going in that head of yours, big brother?" Quinn challenged from across the great room.

"I'm fine." Alex wandered into the kitchen to pour a cup of coffee.

But in truth, he felt numb.

It was over, and not just his relationship with Nicole. The chief might be forced into early retirement, Alex could lose his job, and he'd never see Nicole again.

Not that he wanted to see her, see his own failure reflected back at him when he looked into her eyes. She'd made the right choice: a team of FBI agents over one cop who couldn't even protect his little brother.

"You're going to that crazy place," Quinn said, stepping up with the coffeepot. "I can see it in your eyes."

"It's called a reality check, Quinn."

"Really?" he challenged as Billy joined them in the kitchen. "What does that look like, Alex?"

"She saw me fail over and over again. It was time to cut her losses."

"Stop talking like that. Billy, tell him."

Alex glanced at Billy.

"Nicole made a deal with the FBI agent— she'd come in voluntarily if they released Quinn and left you alone."

Alex clicked into that analytical place, the place where he couldn't feel anything. "She negotiated with the FBI and won. Impressive."

"That's it? That's all you have to say?" Quinn pushed.

"I should contact the Feds and see if they'll work with me on the Lange murder."

He pulled out his phone. Quinn yanked it out of his hand. "Didn't you hear what Billy said? Nicole made a deal. She sacrificed herself for you."

"Survival is not a sacrifice. Besides, she sacrificed herself for both of us."

"Alex, she really cares about you."

"Yeah, whatever. Give me the phone."

Quinn didn't move. He studied Alex as if he were a complete stranger.

"Quinn, the phone," Alex demanded.

Quinn placed it on the kitchen counter. "I don't get you, man."

"What else is new?"

Quinn shook his head and went into the great room.

Alex picked up his phone and hesitated, still processing the fact that Nicole was gone.

"I'm sorry, Alex," Billy said.

Alex glanced up. "You care about my brother. You'll never have to apologize for that."

"I know, but I'm sorry Nicole left. It's just...she was so worried about what it was doing to you when Quinn was taken."

"And now my brother is home so we have a lot to be grateful for." He forced a smile. "If you'll excuse me, I need to make a call."

He went into the office and flopped down in the desk chair. Glancing to his left he spotted the wooden chair Nicole had occupied when they'd gone through video and news stories about Abigail Woods. Nicole's essence still lingered in the room, taunting him, spiking the ache in his chest. She was just here.

And now she was gone.

Leaning back in his chair, Alex resigned himself to the fact that Nicole had made the right decision. On some level he was proud of her for looking out for herself.

Even if that meant abandoning Alex.

She knows what you are. She knows you can't protect her.

Then again, maybe he could. By solving the Lange murder, he'd remove Nicole from the killer's sights. He owed her that much.

He dug Agent Banks's business card out of his wallet and eyed it. Now that the Feds had what they wanted—Nicole—Agent Banks might work with the Waverly Harbor P.D. to solve the murder case.

He told himself he wasn't calling to check on Nicole, to confirm she'd made it safely into FBI custody. This was strictly a business call.

"Banks," the agent answered.

"This is Detective Donovan."

"What, didn't your brother make it home?"

"He's here. Not sure why it was necessary to take him into custody, but whatever."

"He needed an attitude adjustment. He assaulted one of my agents."

"And Chief Roth? You took him into custody because…?"

"He was never in official custody. He voluntarily came in to answer questions. He left about an hour ago."

"I think it's about time to shelve the egos and work together. Sharing information could help us solve our respective cases faster."

"I'm open to that. Do you have any leads in the murder case?"

"Abigail Woods has moved to the top of my suspect list."

Silence filled the line. "Mrs. Woods and I were just discussing the possibility of her brother having a secret life."

"She's in your office?"

"Yes."

"Let me guess, she was the one that suggested Edward had a secret life?"

"I would agree with that, yes."

"You should know she was scheduled to meet with Edward the afternoon he was killed. She could have been the last person to see him alive."

"Did you inquire about that?" Agent Banks asked.

"I haven't had the opportunity. Now that I can focus on the murder case instead of protecting a witness things should run more smoothly."

"I'd appreciate you keeping me in the loop."

"You're willing to work together?"

"Yes, I think it would benefit everyone involved."

"I'll clear it with the chief."

Alex was about to hang up, but had to ask the question.

"So, is Miss Harris safely in your custody?"

"Soon. I sent my team to meet up with her. I expect them shortly."

"Are you going to consider witness protection?"

Which meant Alex would truly never see her again.

"Not at this time, but perhaps in the future."

"Okay, I'll be in touch." Alex ended the call and his connection to Nicole. From this point on he'd have to go through the FBI to question her, which was probably best for everyone involved. The barrier of the federal agency would be a constant reminder that theirs was a professional relationship, not a personal one.

Alex called Chief Roth's home and Gayle answered.

"Hi Gayle, it's Alex."

"He was just about to call you."

"Alex? You okay?" Chief Roth asked.

"I'm fine, sir. How's the gunshot wound?"

"Ah, just a scratch."

Gayle shouted something in the background.

"It's been a wild couple of days, Alex."

"Yes, sir, it has. I'd like to get back on the Lange murder case."

"You were never officially on leave, Alex, you know that."

"Thanks."

"I'd like you to continue protecting the witness," the chief said. "She's our best lead to the killer."

"She chose to go into FBI custody. I just got off the phone with Agent Banks. With your approval I'd like to officially work with the FBI. Maybe we can actually help each other and solve this thing instead of fighting for control."

"Alex?"

"Sir?"

"Do you think it was the best decision for Nicole to go into FBI custody?"

"It wasn't my call. She left without consulting me."

"Oh." He paused. "You two had a fight?"

"No, sir. She left and I think she made the right decision by putting her safety first. I can't fault her for that."

"She should have talked to you first."

"So, are you comfortable with me working with the FBI?" Alex changed the subject.

"Yes, you have my approval. Agent Banks told me that Lange was developing security software for the FBI and was suspected of creating a back door so he would have permanent access, or something like that. Computer stuff isn't my thing."

"Why would he need to have access to their files?"

"He wouldn't, unless he planned to do something criminal with that information. The FBI considered his actions a threat to homeland security. You can see why they were being tight-lipped about it, why they wanted to know everything Miss Harris knew about Edward Lange."

"They seem open to working with us now that they have her in custody."

"She's the key to everything, Alex."

He couldn't argue with that. She surely held the key to Alex's heart.

"What leads are you pursuing?" the chief asked.

"Abigail Woods was on Edward's schedule for the afternoon of his death and now she's trying to convince Agent Banks that her brother had a secret life."

"You think she could have hired someone to kill her brother?"

"It's a possibility."

"But what does that have to do with the back door access stuff?"

"I intend to find out, sir."

"Okay, well, I'll be at home recuperating for a few days."

"A week to ten days!" Gayle shouted in the background.

"Sounds like Gayle's got everything under control," Alex joked.

"You have no idea. Be careful, son."

"Will do."

"And Alex?"

"Sir?"

"Don't give up."

"I won't, thanks."

Alex ended the call and glanced out the front window. Of course he wouldn't give up. Edward Lange deserved justice and vindication. Alex did not believe Edward was involved in terrorist activities against his own country.

Don't give up.

Alex realized the chief wasn't just talking about the case.

He was talking about Nicole.

Alex would like nothing more than to spend time with Nicole outside of work, outside of the danger that trailed them these past few days. He believed in his heart they were blessed with something special.

Something he shouldn't pursue. She deserved someone better, someone who could protect and love her. He hoped God would bless her with such a man.

As the grief of letting her go squeezed his heart, Alex struggled to refocus on the murder case. Yet he wouldn't be able to fully concentrate until he said a prayer for Nicole.

He closed his eyes and took a deep breath. *Lord, please keep her safe. She's a spe-*

*cial woman who's had her share of trials.
She may not realize it, but she needs Your
strength to see her through.*

Footsteps pounded through the house, followed by raised voices. Alex went to investigate and found Quinn sitting in the sofa in
the great room. Billy stood over him, hands
on her hips.

"You can't tell me what to do," she said.

"What's going on?" Alex asked.

"She saw a state patrol car pull into her
driveway and she wants to run over there
and investigate."

"It's my house and I'm going to find out
what's going on." Billy marched toward the
front door.

"Haven't we had enough drama?" Quinn
said, following her. "Come on, Billy. Just
stay here."

Alex followed them outside, ready to flash
his badge.

As Quinn argued with Billy, Alex realized his little brother was being awfully protective of his friend. They definitely shared
something special. He wondered how long
it would take Quinn to figure that out, aban-

don his aloof ways and accept that his feelings for Billy ran deeper than friendship. Then again, Quinn probably didn't want to let any woman get close. He'd seen what falling in love had done to their father and didn't want to make that same disastrous mistake.

Even though Alex had loved Jessica he'd never let the protective wall down completely. Yet with Nicole the wall had never gone up.

"Can I help you?" Billy called out to the state trooper.

The trooper, who looked to be in his thirties, stepped off Billy's porch and joined them at the security gate bordering Quinn's property.

"That's my house," Billy said. "Is there a problem?"

"Are you Wilhelma Renee Bronson?" the trooper asked.

Quinn snorted at the use of her full name.

"I am." She glared at Quinn.

"Are you the registered owner of a 2009 White Volkswagen Jetta?"

A chill ran down Alex's spine.

"Yes, why?" Billy said.

"Your car's been in an accident."

Alex took a step forward and flashed his badge, his hand trembling. "I'm Detective Donovan, Waverly Harbor P.D. Was anyone hurt?"

"No, sir. There was no one in the car."

"Are you all right?"

Nicole looked up into the somewhat familiar eyes of David Woods, Edward's brother-in-law.

"David? What are you doing here?"

Gripping her arm, he pulled her toward a black sedan.

"I've gotta get you out of here. He could come back." He glanced nervously up and down the road.

"I'm supposed to meet the FBI."

"I'll take you. Get in the car," he ordered.

He opened the back door and motioned her inside. "Lay down so they don't see you. Who's trying to hurt you, anyway?"

"I have no idea." She climbed into the sedan and ducked down.

David slid behind the wheel and pulled away from the scene.

"My phone, I need my phone," she said, sitting up.

"Is it worth your life? Come on, lay down."

She flopped down on the seat. Talk about good timing, she'd been lucky David had been driving by.

"Did you see what happened?" she asked.

"He hit you and drove off. It didn't look random to me."

"No, it didn't feel random."

"Where's your meeting?"

"Merriweather Crossing. We're close, right?"

"I think so. I'll put it in my GPS."

"Thank you so much."

"Are you kidding? You're helping them find Edward's killer, right? I mean, you're their only witness."

"Not much of a witness, I'm afraid. I didn't see anything."

"But you heard something?"

"Arguing, mostly. Nothing that's been helpful."

"The killer must not know that. I heard there's been multiple attempts on your life."

"You heard right." And if it hadn't been for Alex, she would have been dead by now.

Alex. She squeezed the strap of her messenger bag and took a deep breath. She hoped he understood why she left. Maybe she should have discussed it with him, but she couldn't risk him talking her out of it. So determined to do the right thing, and in such a hurry so she wouldn't change her mind, she forgot to leave him a note. She'd have to write him one when she got into FBI custody explaining her decision.

"So you didn't hear anything that could help the cops solve the murder case?" David pressed.

"Unfortunately, no."

"Then why are you going into FBI custody?"

The truth was too personal: she'd do anything to protect Alex and ease his pain.

"They requested I come in to help them with something, I don't know what."

"You have no idea?" he asked.

"Nope. Do you think it's safe to sit up yet?"

"Sure."

Nicole glanced out the window, reconsidering her decision to go to the FBI. She hugged herself and realized she'd only felt safe when she was with Alex. But was that love, or some warped type of dependence? A shudder ran down her back.

"Hey, don't worry." David stretched his arm across the seat and smiled. "Everything's going to be okay."

And that's when she noticed the gold bracelet on his right wrist. The same bracelet they'd found in the evidence box.

FIFTEEN

Alex didn't even remember how he got to the scene of the abandoned car. He was at his brother's cabin one minute, and pulling up behind Billy's ditched Jetta the next. Panic spiked through his body at the sight of the dented fender.

He was out of the car before Quinn came to a complete stop. As Alex approached the vehicle the first thing he noticed was that the airbag wasn't deployed. A good thing. So maybe she wasn't hurt.

But what happened and where did she go?

Agent Banks pulled onto the shoulder in front of Billy's car and got out. "Where is she?"

"Don't know. We just got here."

Banks marched up to the driver's side of the car and Alex went to the passenger side.

He whipped open the door and spotted her cell phone. "She wouldn't leave her phone. We have to assume she was taken," he said, trying to keep his emotional distance.

"Or she ran." Banks looked over the top of the car at Alex. "Did you consider that?"

"No. I guarantee you, that did not happen."

"You guarantee me?"

"She wouldn't have run." Not the Nicole he knew. Sure, immediately after Edward's death she'd wanted to run, escape the threat to her life. But she'd changed in the past few days. She'd developed strength and resilience, two traits Alex admired, especially given what she'd been through.

"So if she didn't run, what's your theory?" Banks asked.

Alex dreaded considering it but had no choice. "I've thought all along that she has something or knows something the killer wants, which would explain why he's been after her since the murder."

"Or he just wants her dead."

Panic burned through Alex's gut as he struggled to ignore the agent's words. The thought of never holding her again, kissing her...

"Detective?"

Alex snapped his attention to Agent Banks.

"You want to share with the class?" the agent said.

Alex turned and walked back to Quinn's SUV.

"Hey, what about us working together?" Banks called after him.

"The deal's still on. I'm going to interview Abigail Woods."

He got into the SUV and slammed the door.

"Well?" Quinn asked.

"Can you take me to my car?" Alex asked.

"Sure, Billy has to wait for a tow. Let me tell her the plan." Quinn got out and went over to Billy, who hovered beside the ditched car.

One thing was for sure—Alex had to tamp down the dread flooding his body. Focus was key if he stood a chance of finding Nicole.

But would he find her alive?

He fisted his hand and slammed it against

his thigh. He had to think positive. He had to find her.

Because the thought of never seeing her again…

"Stop, just stop," he hushed.

His phone rang and he recognized the P.D.'s number. "Donovan."

"It's Wendy. A woman called the station looking for you. Her name is Ruby and she said she was on the phone with Nicole when a car bumped her from behind."

"Did she leave a number?"

Wendy gave him the number and he immediately called Nicole's friend.

"This is Ruby."

"This is Alex Donovan. I—"

"Are you the one who's been taking care of Nicole?"

"I am," he said, fighting back the shame of doing a poor job of it.

"She told me to find you if anything weird happened. I asked her what that meant and she screamed and then she was gone."

"She screamed?" Alex repeated, every muscle in his body tensing up.

"Yeah, like a scream of surprise, then I

heard her say, 'David, what are you doing here?'"

Alex squeezed the phone so hard he thought it might crack. "David Woods?"

"She didn't say a last name. And then she was gone. You've gotta find her."

"That's the plan. Thank you, Ruby. I'll be in touch."

Quinn got back into the car. "I'll meet Billy in town at Jake's Garage."

"It's David Woods."

Quinn stared at him. "Edward's brother-in-law?"

Alex nodded. "I've got to find them, Quinn. I've got to find Abigail and her husband."

"Well you're in luck. They're renting a room at The Sandpiper."

Alex called for Officer Mark Adams to join him at the lodge. The front desk clerk said Abigail Woods and a small group of friends were in a conference room analyzing calls they'd received from people who'd phoned the tip line.

Quinn led Alex to the conference room

and stopped outside the door. "I've got to take care of some business."

"Thanks, little brother."

"Alex?"

"Yeah?"

"You'll find her." Quinn reached out and hugged Alex.

Quinn hadn't intentionally hugged Alex since…Alex struggled to remember the last time they hugged like this and realized it was the day of their mother's funeral.

Quinn let go and took off down the hall. Alex watched him for a second, wishing he could have said *thanks* or *I love you, little brother.* Instead, he turned to the conference room door.

"How do you want to work this?" Officer Adams asked.

"I need to talk to Abigail and David Woods alone. I'll ask everyone to leave and you guard the door."

"Yes, sir."

Abigail and David Woods. If they were both behind this door that meant Nicole could be gone for good, probably dead at the bottom of the lake. If David wasn't in the room, he could be with Nicole trying to extract the information he needed from her.

Alex pushed open the door. Half a dozen people looked up. David Woods was not one of them. Relief warred with desperation in Alex's chest.

"I need to speak with Abigail, alone."

"Good. I have to speak with you, too, detective," Abigail said. "I'm demanding your resignation."

"Everyone, please excuse us," Alex said, ignoring her.

Officer Adams herded two men and three women out of the room. The door shut with a deafening click.

"I'm doing more to find my brother's killer than your entire department's done in the past few days. I can't believe how—"

"Stop the dramatics and tell me where your husband is."

"David? Why?"

"He's our prime suspect."

"That just shows how incompetent you are."

Alex stepped closer. "I don't appreciate games, Abigail. I know your husband has

Nicole and if you don't tell me where he is I'm charging you with obstruction."

She flopped down in a nearby chair. "You're serious."

"Someone's been after Nicole Harris since your brother's death. Either the killer thinks she can identify him, or Nicole has something the killer wants. A few hours ago Nicole was taken against her will by your husband. The question is how involved are you?"

"You're wrong. David would never hurt anyone," she said, suddenly breathless.

"Where was he the night of Edward's murder?"

"Vancouver. On a business trip."

"Did he call you from a hotel? Can he prove he was there?"

"No, and I didn't think he'd need to prove—"

"Was he involved with Tech-Link?"

"Yes, he was on the software development team, why?"

"My theory is that the Tech-Link software was a threat to national security. That's why the FBI is involved."

"And you think David is a part of this?" Her voice raised a pitch.

"Yes, ma'am. I suspect you're involved, as well."

"That's ridiculous!"

"You were quick to accuse Nicole of killing your brother, you put up reward money to complicate the investigation with false leads and you suggested that Edward had a secret life. These can be seen as distractions from the real perpetrator."

She glanced down at her hands and he thought he might have broken her. When she didn't say anything, he kept pushing.

"Nicole is a good person who doesn't deserve to be collateral damage. Help me find her or I will charge you with obstruction."

She snapped her eyes to his. "I had nothing to do with any of this. I wanted to vindicate my brother by finding his killer."

"Why did you suggest he led a secret life?"

She sighed. "When I discovered certain things about him after his death, it made me realize how little I knew about him, my own brother." She glanced at Alex. "I guess the only way I could deal with that was to assume he had a secret life."

"What was your husband's relationship like with your brother?"

She looked up. "Good, until recently. David and my brother were butting heads about a new software product. David said he wanted to work it out, but my brother wouldn't return his calls. When I asked Edward about it he'd promise to talk to David."

"So, you didn't know what the product was?"

"No."

Alex studied her as she processed the accusation that her husband could be her brother's killer.

"I think we both know your brother well enough to assume he wouldn't want an innocent woman to be killed because of his work."

"She's not innocent. Nicole was there, she could have stopped it!"

"She was traumatized."

"Right, the traumatized girl with the criminal past. David and I knew about her being arrested for beating up her father, how there were multiple police calls to her childhood home. David told me she has severe mental problems, posttraumatic, whatever. I don't care. She could help us find Edward's killer but she won't."

"She doesn't deserve to die. Isn't that what your husband plans to do to her? Kill her?"

"No, no." She stood and paced to the other side of the room. "I can't believe David is involved. She's not with him. You're wrong."

But he read panic in her eyes as she grappled with the truth.

"Then help me clear his name by telling me where he is," Alex said.

She pulled a business card out of her suit jacket pocket. "He was going to look at a rental this afternoon. We weren't sure how long we'd have to stay in Waverly Harbor so we decided to rent a house. The address is on the back of the card."

"Officer Adams will take you back to the station."

"I'd rather stay here and continue to work on finding my brother's killer, if that's okay with you," she said in soft voice.

Her world was crumbling with the possi-

bility that her husband had viciously murdered her brother.

"If a lead implicates your husband I'll expect you to share it with us," Alex said.

"Of course," she said, with surrender in
her voice.

Alex sensed that somewhere, deep down,
she'd accepted the truth about her husband
but clung to hope that he was innocent.

Alex opened the door and motioned for
Officer Adams. "Stay with Abigail until you
hear from me."

Alex, Agent Banks and his team surrounded the rental house. Banks motioned
for his three agents to cover the sides and
back of the house in case David tried to escape through a window. Banks and Alex
took the front.

"I appreciate the call," Banks said as they
approached the porch.

"Yep." Alex's mind was elsewhere, focused on what was happening inside. Fear
burned through his chest at what he thought
he might find.

They sneaked onto the porch and Banks pounded on the door. "FBI, open the door!"

A crash echoed from inside the house. Banks nodded at Alex, who took a step back and kicked the door once, twice.

It swung open and he aimed his gun....

At a middle-aged woman wearing a blue suit. He blew past her, letting the Feds deal with her while Alex searched the house. He raced up the stairs to check all three bedrooms. He slid open closet doors and looked behind shower curtains in the two bathrooms.

The place was empty except for the woman in the living room. Beating back the dread simmering in his gut, Alex went downstairs.

"You had an appointment with David Woods at what time?" Banks questioned the woman, who sat on the sofa clutching her hands in her lap.

"We were supposed to meet at three o'clock, then he called and said an emergency came up but I have another appointment at four so I thought I'd wait," she rambled.

"I'm sorry that we startled you," Agent

Banks said, eyeing the broken vase on the floor.

"Did he give you any indication where this emergency was? Where he was going?" Alex tried.

"No. Sorry."

Alex holstered his gun and went outside. He couldn't stand to be in this house, so close to finding her, to saving Nicole only to hit another dead end. He wondered if this wild goose chase had been intentional on Abigail's part. Yet, she'd looked genuinely shocked when Alex accused David of kidnapping Nicole.

No, this was all David Woods. He needed something from Nicole and as long as she didn't give it to him she'd stay alive.

Yet David would do anything to get it out of her. Alex fisted his hand. Would the monster beat her, like her father? Physical abuse would make her shut down for sure, and then David wouldn't be able to get anything out of her. If David were smart he'd apply mental pressure.

David told me she has severe mental problems, posttraumatic, whatever.

What better place to apply emotional pressure than to take her back to the scene of Edward's murder?

"Banks!" Alex called.

The agent jogged across the property.

"Have you got men at Lange's lake house?" Alex asked.

"No, why?"

Alex whipped open his car door. "Because I'm guessing that's where he's taken her."

When David turned onto the lake road Nicole feared she had minutes to live. If David was Edward's killer, he'd been trying to hurt or kill Nicole since the night of the murder. Or at least kidnap her.

Somehow she needed to stall him long enough for Alex to find her.

Really, Nic? You walked out on him without so much as a note. How is he going to find you?

They pulled up to the gates of Edward's lake house. "Since I couldn't find Merriweather Crossing I figured there'd be police officers here who could protect you better than I."

Oh, wasn't he clever.

Edward pressed the code, the gates opened and he pulled up to the house. Her pulse raced with the memory of the night Edward Lange was murdered. Images filled her brain: shouting, crashing and blood.

So much blood.

She realized that's what he was hoping for. He wanted Nicole weak and broken, traumatized to the point where she'd give him what he needed. She wondered what it was.

She knew the moment she gave it to him he'd no doubt kill her. Probably slit her wrists and make it look as if she'd committed suicide.

With his briefcase slung over his shoulder, David pulled down the yellow tape blocking the door and motioned her inside.

"Thank you so much." She smiled, hoping he had no clue she was onto him.

"Hello!" he called out. "Any law enforcement here?"

Silence echoed back at them.

"Strange," he said. "Well, as long as we're here, maybe you could help me with something."

"What's that?"

"Abigail and I were discussing the murder the other night." He motioned her into the office.

She froze in the doorway. "I...I don't think I can go in there."

"Just for a second?"

Then she remembered the alarm button beneath the desk that connected directly to the Waverly P.D. If she could get to it without David knowing...

"Okay." As she wandered into the office, heat crawled up her neck to her cheeks. The room smelled of dried blood and death, and she could picture Edward laying facedown on the floor.

David placed his hand on her back and led her across the room to the closet. Her heartbeat pounded in her ears as she drowned in violent images.

"It must have been horrible for you to be sitting on the other side of this door." He tapped on the wood with his knuckles. "The things you must have heard...."

Nicole was falling deeper, deeper into the abyss.

Which is exactly what he wants.

"Are you all right?" he asked in a saccharine sweet voice.

She couldn't answer. She just stared at the door, a war raging inside of her. As she kept telling herself she was not a victim, her father's words hounded her: *you will never be safe.*

Then another voice rose to the surface.

Well, look at you.

It was Alex's voice when she'd fisted her hands, ready to take on the intruder at the mill. He'd been proud of her courage, her newfound strength.

The memory of his voice pulled her out of her spiral. She had to get to the desk and press the alarm button without raising suspicion.

David expected her to be fragile so she'd play along. Then, after she pressed the button she'd work up to using the Donovan Slam and escape.

She placed a dramatic hand to her chest. "I think I need to sit down."

"Of course." Cupping her elbow, David led her to the desk chair.

Perfect. The button was within reach.

"I'm sorry, it was wrong of me to bring you in here but I've got this problem and I need your help," David said.

She gazed at him, pretending to be disoriented.

"The Lange Industries all access network pass code, do you have it?"

"Yes."

As he pulled a laptop out of his briefcase, she reached beneath the desk and pressed the alarm. Now she just had to survive the three to five minutes it would take for authorities to get here.

She couldn't believe how comfortable David was in the very room where he'd violently killed his brother-in-law. But then, psychopaths didn't feel anything like empathy or remorse.

Yet remorse filled her chest at the thought that she may never see Alex again.

Eyeing his laptop, David asked, "What's the pass code?"

"I'm not supposed to tell anyone or I could lose my job."

He cracked a smile that made her skin crawl. "Not to worry. That won't happen."

Yeah, because I'll be dead.

"Why do you need it?" she innocently asked.

"I have a project that Edward was in the process of approving, and I need to know if that happened before he…" David glanced at his computer screen and pretended to fight back a moment of grief.

Once she gave him the pass code her life was over. Not that she'd ever give him the real pass code.

"I understand your reticence. You hardly know me. It's all about trust, isn't it?" He placed his hand on her shoulder.

She closed her eyes.

"We should get to know each other better. I understand your sister, Adeline, started a new job as a school counselor in Marysville. How is she liking it?"

"Fine, thank you," she said, recognizing the insidious threat to her family.

"I'm not sure about the neighborhood she moved into. Did you help her choose it?"

"No."

"Well, I'd hate for anything to happen to her. Your family has been through enough."

He squeezed her shoulder.

Nicole broke the connection by wandering to the window. *Stall, girl, buy time.*

"Do you have brothers and sisters?" she asked.

"Yes, one of each. Family is so important, don't you think?"

"Very."

"Then why haven't you spoken with your brother in more than a year?"

She spun around. "How do you know that?"

He shrugged. "I also know he's been in an alcohol recovery program." He stalked toward her. "I know he's struggling to keep his job as a police officer, that he lost the love of his life to a better man. I know he passes a pub every day on his way home from work."

"You know more than I do." She stared out the window.

"I also know that you've grown close to Detective Donovan in the past few days. I understand he's had a rough time, what with his girlfriend and his father dying in the same year. Must be hard to lose every-one you care about. It's just a matter of time before his little brother gets killed in a thrill-seeking adventure."

Losing Quinn would destroy Alex.

"Quinn's a smart man. He can take care of himself," she said.

"You think so?" David pulled out his phone. "It's David. Take care of Quinn Donovan for me, will you?" He pocketed his phone.

"What are you doing?" she said.

"No more games. Give me the code and I'll retract my order."

"Who was that?"

"A loyal employee." He wandered back to the computer. "A mercenary who knows how to terminate a problem."

Quinn. They were going to terminate Quinn.

God, no.

"The pass code?" he prompted.

She couldn't trust that David would cancel his order to have Quinn killed.

"Cancel what you just did," she said.

"After you give me the pass code."

"Six, four, seven, two, nine, eight, four," she lied.

She had to get out of here, warn Alex that his brother's life was in danger.

When the numbers didn't work, he slammed his fist on the desk and glared at her. "Are you messing with me?"

"What? It should work."

He tried again. She glanced out the window. Where were the cops?

"Do you think I'm stupid? Who else has to die because of your stubbornness?"

"I can't help it if you can't type."

He marched toward her, his eyes glaring.

He wouldn't kill her until he had the code, but he'd continue to hurt the people she loved.

Unless she stopped him. *Please, God, help me be strong. Help me protect the people I love.*

He reached out to grab her.

"No!" She swung the heel of her palm against his chest—left, right, left—and slammed her palm up to connect with his nose.

He cried out and grabbed his nose, stumbling backward.

Nicole shoved him to the ground and sprinted for the door.

SIXTEEN

She was halfway down the driveway when gunshots vibrated against her eardrums. She hit the ground and glanced left, looking for a place to take cover.

Tires squealed as three cars sped up the driveway.

"Stay down!" Alex called out to her.

A few more shots were fired, then silence. Heart pounding against her chest, she looked up as Alex kneeled beside her.

"You're okay, right?" he said. "Tell me you're okay."

"I did it, Alex. I did the Donovan Slam and got away."

"I'm so proud of you." He hugged her.

"Quinn's in trouble." She broke the hug. "David made a call. Ordered someone to hurt Quinn."

Alex helped her stand and pulled the phone off his belt to call Quinn. When she glanced toward the house, he put his arm around her and led her away.

"You've seen enough," he said, then directed his attention to the phone call. "Quinn, we got David Woods, but Nicole said he ordered someone to come after you. We'll trace the call but in the meantime… I'd rather you not… Just stay where you are. Why are you fighting me on this?"

He held out the phone and stared at it. "Stubborn kid." He glanced at the FBI team swarming the property. "Banks!"

Alex redirected his attention to Nicole. A warm, relieved smile played at his lips. "I'm so sorry. I should have been here."

She thought he might kiss her; she wanted him to kiss her. Everything she'd done had been to protect herself and Alex in the hopes of pursuing something real together, a future.

"I'm going to have an agent get you out of here."

"Alex, I—"

"David Woods is still alive," Agent Banks

said, approaching them. "Ambulance is on the way."

"Can someone take Nicole back to the station?"

"Alex, I want to stay with you."

He looked deep into her eyes. "Please, sweetheart. I'll be able to focus better if I know you're tucked safely away."

She nodded.

"I've gotta check David's phone. Nicole said he sent someone after my brother," Alex said.

Agent Banks waved a young agent over. "Masterson!"

All the activity and shouting was giving her a headache. Or maybe it was the tension building in her chest for the past hour, the stress of thinking she'd never see Alex again. Never kiss him again or feel his arms around her.

A tall, blond agent joined them.

"This is Agent Masterson," Agent Banks introduced.

"Hi," Nicole greeted.

"I'll catch up with you later." Alex squeezed her hand.

When he let go, a chill flooded her chest and her legs weakened, but she forced herself to remain strong for Alex.

"Go on," she said.

Alex took off toward the house and she had an odd feeling that she was never going to see him again. The agent led her to the waiting Suburban.

"Nicole!" Alex called out.

She turned and he smiled at her. "I'll see you back at the station."

She watched him disappear into the house. It was as if he'd read her mind or felt her trepidation about being apart from him.

In that moment she realized how emotionally connected they truly were.

Alex didn't stop by the police station that night. Even though Agent Banks said Alex was fine, Quinn was safe and all was well, she felt anything but calm.

She stayed at the Harbor Lights Inn for a few days while the FBI continued its investigation. Each day she hoped, expected Alex to show up.

He didn't.

Nicole's life had been threatened numerous times yet that didn't scare her nearly as much as the thought of losing Alex. Had she done something to drive him away?

Perhaps she was overreacting and he was busy wrapping up the case.

Finally, on the day she was scheduled to leave town, Alex showed up at the inn. She was sitting on the front porch, hoping, praying he'd show up and talk her out of heading back to Seattle.

"Hey, you," she said, reaching out to him.

He ignored the gesture and sat on a porch chair next to her. A chill raced down her spine.

"I've been worried about you," she said.

"Sorry, it's been a crazy few days." He glanced across the front yard, avoiding eye contact. "Had to wrap everything up."

"David Woods was behind it all?" she asked, wishing he'd look at her.

"Yep. Apparently he killed Edward during a fight over the security program. Edward put David in charge of developing the software but David created the back door access and Edward found out. What you heard was David trying to convince his brother-in-law that the back door access was a good idea."

"And he was after me for the daily pass code, but why?"

"We think to cover his tracks. Delete emails and text messages off Edward's email and phone that would implicate him. David broke into Harbor Lights Inn that night looking for your smartphone in the hopes of finding the pass code."

"And he bumped us off the road the night we were headed to the mill?"

"Actually that was a thug named Ray Patterson, hired by David to get you out of police custody. Ray was also the phony FBI agent who tried to take you from the medical center."

"But why kill Artie?"

"David paid Artie to tell him where Ed-

ward would be at any given time. That's how
he knew he was at the lake house. Artie suspected David might be the killer, so David
had him eliminated. David also had Ray
take a shot at the chief and me, hoping to
distract us while David went looking for
you. Being exceptionally tech savvy, David
cloned Agent Banks's phone, which is how
he knew you were coming into FBI custody
in Billy's Jetta. Ray bumped you off the road
so David could get you alone and coerce you
into giving up the pass code."

"He knew a lot of stuff about my brother
and sister."

"We've traced calls to a few private inves-
tigators he no doubt hired to dig up information about your family."

"Did the FBI shut down the software?"

"They did, with help from Gerry Walker,
one of my original suspects, who was on the
development team."

"Why create the back door access in the
first place?"

"What we've pieced together is that David

resented Edward's success, and the way Abigail admired him. So in one swift move David could make millions by selling the information to U.S. enemies, pin the blame on Edward and destroy his life."

"That's a lot of hate."

A moment of silence passed between them.

"You played a big part in both cases," Alex said. "You should be proud of yourself."

"Well, I didn't do it alone. I had you, and I had my faith."

He finally glanced at her. "Your faith?"

"When David was threatening me at the lake house I felt so vulnerable, so alone. Then I realized I wasn't alone. I said a prayer, Alex, and it gave me strength."

"I'm so glad."

"Of course, my first instinct was to pray for you to come save me."

He cracked a sad smile and stood. "I'd better get back."

"Alex?" She got up and took a step toward him.

"Don't."

He shook his head and she went cold all over.

When he glanced into her eyes her breath caught at the pain she saw there.

"Be safe," he said.

She struggled to breathe as she watched the love of her life walk away.

Alex kept busy for the next few days, drank a lot of coffee and started running again, hoping to ease the ache in his chest.

Nothing worked. Still, he wouldn't allow himself to regret his decision. It's not like he had a choice. He loved Nicole and she was better off with a man who could protect her, not a failure like Alex who was incapable of protecting the people closest to him.

Alex went to check on Quinn who, for some mysterious reason, was dodging his calls. Alex hoped that's all it was and Quinn hadn't gotten himself into trouble. He pulled up to Quinn's secluded home and spotted his brother outside with a female, not Billy.

"Quinn! Open the gate!" Alex called out.

Instead, Quinn led the woman around the back of the house, out of view.

Suddenly the gates opened and Alex pulled up the drive. Billy opened the front door and greeted him.

"Billy, good to see you," Alex said and gave her a hug.

"You, too. I was just finishing up some things at the house before I took off."

"You're leaving?"

"I was offered a job up in Bellingham."

"Why'd you let him in here?" Quinn said, coming around the corner.

"He's your brother," she snapped.

"I'm not talking to him right now."

"What did I do?" Alex said.

"I don't talk to stupid people."

"And your blonde friend, what, has a Ph.D. in physics?"

"We're not talking about her."

"At least that's something," Billy muttered.

"Then what are we talking about, Quinn?"

"What you did to Nicole."

"I did her a favor."

"Right, ripping her heart out is doing her a favor. See what I mean? Stupid."

"Hey, my relationship with Nicole is none of your—"

"Do you know how many times she's called me?" Quinn interrupted. "Trying to figure out what she'd done?"

"What she'd done?"

"Yeah, to make you abandon her. I finally had to ask her to stop calling. Do you know how that made me feel?"

"It's not like you haven't ignored women before."

Quinn lunged at Alex and they tumbled off the porch onto the front yard. They rolled and punched, and Alex realized he wasn't angry with his brother.

He was furious with himself.

In the process of trying to do the right thing for Nicole, he'd hurt her.

The shock of cold water made Alex gasp. He and Quinn froze and looked up.

Billy stood over them with the hose.

"Okay, now that you've got that out of your system, shake hands and make up."

They stood and Alex extended his hand but Quinn shook his head. "Not until you talk to her."

"I did the right thing, Quinn. I'm no good for her."

"You can't keep taking the blame for everything, Alex. It's not your fault a killer was after her, or that Jessica was killed, or that Sophia cleaned out Dad's bank accounts. None of it's your fault." Quinn took a step closer. "The only thing that's your fault is breaking that woman's heart. You guys are good for each other and you know it, but you're going to punish yourself because…" Quinn waved his hand in dismissal. "Get off my property."

He turned and marched away.

"Oh, Mr. Donovan!" A female voice echoed from the backyard.

Soaked through to the skin, Alex stood there, watching his little brother walk away.

Is that what Alex had been doing? Taking the blame for everything? Punishing himself?

"I thought I was doing the right thing," he whispered. "I didn't mean to hurt her."

"I know." Billy sighed, glancing toward the backyard. "You guys never do."

Fearing Nicole would refuse to see him, Alex had Ruby schedule an appointment for Nicole to meet a new client—Alex.

Alex waited at a restaurant with a view of Puget Sound in Seattle's Queen Anne neighborhood. Ruby said it was one of Nicole's favorites and Alex could see why. It was a charming Victorian home converted into a restaurant. It reminded him of the Harbor Lights Inn.

He arrived early to get his bearings and spend a few minutes figuring out what he was going to say, how he was going to make this right. First he'd apologize for hurting her. He thought letting her go to find a better man was an act of love, but after some time of reflection and prayer, he realized it was selfish. He was so focused on his own failures that he couldn't see he was hurting Nicole, the woman he loved with all his heart. But could she forgive him for being so dense?

A jingling sound echoed across the room and he glanced up. Nicole stood in the doorway, long red hair flowing across her shoulders, bright and expectant eyes scanning the room. His heart ached with a kind of need he'd only felt when in her presence. She looked…enchanting.

Then she glanced at him and her smile faded. He stood, hoping she wouldn't turn and bolt out the restaurant, leaving him alone with his shame. She took a deep breath and headed toward him.

"Hi," he said.

"What are you doing here? I was supposed to meet… Wait a second." She narrowed her eyes.

He motioned for her to sit down. "Please?"

"Did Ruby set this up?"

"I asked her to, yes. Can we talk?"

With a raised eyebrow she sat down and

slung her messenger bag over the back of the chair. "I thought guys didn't like to talk."

"We don't, but sometimes we have no choice."

"What's going on? Is it about the case?"

"No."

"Quinn's okay?"

"He's a pain in my neck but otherwise fine."

"And Billy—"

"Stop." He took her hand and stroked the back of it with his thumb, marveling at her soft skin. "I'm sorry I couldn't protect you. I wish I were a better man, I wish—"

"What are you talking about?"

"I get that that's why you chose to go with the FBI over staying with me. You wanted to feel safe, something I couldn't provide. It's okay, I get it."

She pulled away and made a T with her hands. "Time out. I went to the FBI because I couldn't stand to see you hurting. They took your brother, Alex. They brought the chief in for questioning. You were hurt deeply through all the people you care about because you were protecting me. I couldn't stand it anymore. That's why I traded myself in for your brother's freedom. There's nothing worse than seeing the person you love in pain."

"I know," he whispered. "And I'm sorry for that, too."

"Hey, hey." She reached out and placed her palm against his cheek. "Weren't you the one that said we all deserve God's love and forgiveness?"

He leaned into her touch, the warmth of her palm easing the tension from his shoulders.

"What did I do to deserve you?" he whispered.

"Do you want the list?" She cracked a half smile. "You're a good man, Alex. It's time to forgive yourself and move on."

He took her hand and brought it to his lips. "You really forgive me?"

"Yes, love, I do. You led me out of the darkness and into the light. You helped me believe again. In God, in love. I love you, Alex Donovan."

She leaned forward and kissed him, her lips soft and warm. He fought the urge to pick her up, carry her to his car and drive back to Waverly Harbor. He broke the kiss and they pressed their foreheads together.

"You're here and I'm in Waverly Harbor," he said. "Think we can make this work?"

"I hear love conquers all."

"I've heard that, too." And today, with Nicole in his arms, Alex actually believed it to be true.

* * * * *

Dear Reader,

Some of us hold on to traumatic childhood memories that affect both our decisions and our relationships. Nicole Harris thinks she's dealt with her abusive childhood when, in fact, she's been on the run since she left home. It takes a violent situation to force her into confronting her fears. With the support of a compassionate police detective and the community of Waverly Harbor, she's able to work through the trauma of her past to come out the other side as a stronger and wiser person.

My hope is that it doesn't take a traumatic situation to make us confront our pasts; that through our belief in God and support of friends and family we can feel safe to explore our emotional wounds that have yet to heal.

We can continue to look away or deny our pain, but no matter how fast we run it will always be right behind us, like a shadow mirroring our every move. Safe Harbor is about confronting emotional pain in a way

that will make us stronger as we focus on
finding our way to Grace.
Wishing you a safe journey…

Peace,
Hope White

Questions for Discussion

1. Do you think Nicole should have fled Waverly Harbor or stayed to help with the police investigation?

2. Do you think Alex was right to assign himself as Nicole's personal protector? Why or why not?

3. Have you ever known someone like Alex who blamed himself for others' misfortunes? If so, how did you help him or her?

4. If you were Nicole, what would you have done to cultivate a relationship with your estranged siblings?

5. Do you think Nicole was effectively managing her life, considering her traumatic upbringing?

6. Have you ever found yourself haunted by your past? Can you think of any Bible passages that could help ease the fear?

7. Do you think less of Alex for leaving home to join the service in order to get away from his abusive stepmother?

8. Did it seem to you that Nicole had been dealing with her childhood trauma or avoiding it? How so?

9. Do you think Alex was right to keep Nicole at an emotional distance during the investigation? Why or why not?

10. What were your opinions about Alex's brother, Quinn?

11. Do you think Alex failed Nicole when he was assaulted by the mystery driver? Should she have gone back to help Alex?

12. Did you agree with Nicole's decision to turn herself in to the FBI? Why or why not?

REQUEST YOUR FREE BOOKS!

2 FREE RIVETING INSPIRATIONAL NOVELS IN TRUE LARGE PRINT PLUS 2 FREE MYSTERY GIFTS

Love Inspired® SUSPENSE

TRUE LARGE PRINT

YES! Please send me 2 FREE Love Inspired® Suspense True Large Print novels and my 2 FREE mystery gifts (gifts are worth about $10). After receiving them, if I don't wish to receive any more books, I can return the shipping statement marked "cancel." If I don't cancel, I will receive 3 brand-new true large print novels every month and be billed just $7.99 per book in the U.S. or $9.99 per book in Canada. That's a savings of at least 33% off the cover price. It's quite a bargain! Shipping and handling is just 50¢ per book in the U.S. and 75¢ per book in Canada.* I understand that accepting the 2 free books and gifts places me under no obligation to buy anything. I can always return the shipment and cancel at any time. Even if I never buy another book, the two free books and gifts are mine to keep forever.

124/324 IDN FV2K

Name _____ (PLEASE PRINT)

Address _____ Apt. #

City _____ State/Prov. _____ Zip/Postal Code

Signature (if under 18, a parent or guardian must sign)

Mail to the Harlequin® Reader Service:
IN U.S.A.: P.O. Box 1867, Buffalo, NY 14240-1867
IN CANADA: P.O. Box 609, Fort Erie, Ontario L2A 5X3

* Terms and prices subject to change without notice. Prices do not include applicable taxes. Sales tax applicable in N.Y. Canadian residents will be charged applicable taxes. Offer not valid in Quebec. This offer is limited to one order per household. Not valid for current subscribers to Love Inspired Suspense True Large Print books. All orders subject to credit approval. Credit or debit balances in a customer's account(s) may be offset by any other outstanding balance owed by or to the customer. Please allow 4 to 6 weeks for delivery. Offer available while quantities last.

Your Privacy—The Harlequin® Reader Service is committed to protecting your privacy. Our Privacy Policy is available online at www.ReaderService.com or upon request from the Harlequin Reader Service.

We make a portion of our mailing list available to reputable third parties that offer products we believe may interest you. If you prefer that we not exchange your name with third parties, or if you wish to clarify or modify your communication preferences, please visit us at www.ReaderService.com/consumerschoice or write to us at Harlequin Reader Service Preference Service, P.O. Box 9062, Buffalo, NY 14269. Include your complete name and address.

REQUEST YOUR FREE BOOKS!

2 FREE INSPIRATIONAL NOVELS IN TRUE LARGE PRINT
PLUS 2 FREE MYSTERY GIFTS

Love Inspired™

TRUE LARGE PRINT

YES! Please send me 2 FREE Love Inspired® True Large Print novels and my 2 FREE mystery gifts (gifts are worth about $10). After receiving them, if I don't wish to receive any more books, I can return the shipping statement marked "cancel." If I don't cancel, I will receive 3 brand-new true large print novels every month and be billed just $7.99 per book in the U.S. or $9.99 per book in Canada. That's a savings of at least 33% off the cover price. It's quite a bargain! Shipping and handling is just 50¢ per book in the U.S. and 75¢ per book in Canada.* I understand that accepting the 2 free books and gifts places me under no obligation to buy anything. I can always return the shipment and cancel at any time. Even if I never buy another book, the two free books and gifts are mine to keep forever.

117/307 IDN FVZK

Name	(PLEASE PRINT)

Address	Apt. #

City	State/Prov.	Zip/Postal Code

Signature (if under 18, a parent or guardian must sign)

Mail to the Harlequin® Reader Service:
IN U.S.A.: P.O. Box 1867, Buffalo, NY 14240-1867
IN CANADA: P.O. Box 609, Fort Erie, Ontario L2A 5X3

* Terms and prices subject to change without notice. Prices do not include applicable taxes. Sales tax applicable in N.Y. Canadian residents will be charged applicable taxes. Offer not valid in Quebec. This offer is limited to one order per household. Not valid for current subscribers to Love Inspired True Large Print books. All orders subject to credit approval. Credit or debit balances in a customer's account(s) may be offset by any other outstanding balance owed by or to the customer. Please allow 4 to 6 weeks for delivery. Offer available while quantities last.

Your Privacy—The Harlequin® Reader Service is committed to protecting your privacy. Our Privacy Policy is available online at www.ReaderService.com or upon request from the Harlequin Reader Service.

We make a portion of our mailing list available to reputable third parties that offer products we believe may interest you. If you prefer that we not exchange your name with third parties, or if you wish to clarify or modify your communication preferences, please visit us at www.ReaderService.com/consumerschoice or write to us at Harlequin Reader Service Preference Service, P.O. Box 9062, Buffalo, NY 14269. Include your complete name and address.

LITLP13TR

ReaderService.com

Manage your account online!

- Review your order history
- Manage your payments
- Update your address

*We've designed
the Harlequin® Reader Service
website just for you.*

Enjoy all the features!

- Reader excerpts from any series
- Respond to mailings and special monthly offers
- Discover new series available to you
- Browse the Bonus Bucks catalogue
- Share your feedback

Visit us at:
ReaderService.com